BIG MATCH MANAGER

BIG MATCH MANAGER

TOM SHELDON

illustrated by
Nathan Burton

BLOOMSBURY
CHILDREN'S
BOOKS

For Kate and Joe

First published in Great Britain in 2004 by Bloomsbury Publishing Plc,
38 Soho Square, London, W1D 3HB

Text copyright © 2004 by Tom Sheldon
Illustrations copyright © 2004 by Nathan Burton
The moral rights of the author and illustrator have been asserted

A CIP record of this book is available from the
British Library

ISBN 0 7475 7335 2

Printed in Great Britain by Clays Ltd, St Ives plc

10 9 8 7 6 5 4 3 2 1

All papers used by Bloomsbury Publishing are natural, recyclable products
made from wood grown in well-managed forests.
The manufacturing processes conform to the environmental
regulations of the country of origin.

Getting Started

This is a book with a difference. You don't open it at page one and keep reading until the end like any other book. Instead, YOU play the central character – and by making decisions as you go along, you change what happens!

In this book, every paragraph has a number. At the end of each paragraph, you may be asked to make a choice – and you will be told which paragraph number to turn to. If you haven't read this kind of book before, don't worry – it's easy once you get started. You will need some basic items before you begin: a pencil, a rubber and a pair of six-sided dice. (If you can't find any dice, you'll notice that at the bottom of every page a pair of dice has been printed. When you are told to roll dice, just open the book at a random page – and there's your dice roll for you.)

In this story you are the manager of Hardwick City Football Club, one of the best teams in the league. There are nine other teams in your league, and you'll play a match against each of them as you progress through the book. But wait – there's a twist. One of your best players has gone missing, and you've got to solve clues as you go along to track him down. More about that in a minute. First it's time to tell you about . . .

The Fact Sheet

Even the best managers can't remember everything, so on page 222 you have been provided with a **Fact Sheet**. This is where you write down all your team information and match results, as well as the clues and objects you collect as you go along. But remember always to use a pencil so you can rub things out if they change, or if you play the book all over again. Remember you can be the Big Match Manager as many times as you like!

You start the season with a **Budget** of 5 million pounds at your disposal. This is so you can buy new players as you go along. Write it in the space at the top of your Fact Sheet now. Five million doesn't go far these days, and sometimes you might decide you want to sell a player to another club to bump up your bank account. You'll be told which players can be bought and sold as you go along. But you must never let your Budget slip below zero. It's in your contract!

Next on the Fact Sheet you'll see your **Fixture List**. This tells you which other teams are in the league with you, and what order you'll be playing them in.

After that come your team's **Morale** and **Fitness**.

Morale describes the general mood of your team. Winning matches and good management help improve **Morale**. **Roll one dice**. (If you're using the dice printed in this book, just use the one on the left.) This number is the Morale you start the book with – you can write it on your Fact Sheet now. Morale will change as you make your way through this book.

Fitness is a measure of how well trained your squad is. Fit and healthy players can run faster on the pitch and recover from injuries more quickly. Roll one dice again – this is the Fitness you start with. Write it on the Fact Sheet. Like Morale, your Fitness level will change as the book goes on.

Your Team

Look further down the Fact Sheet, and you'll see your **Squad Details**. You have eighteen players in your Squad to choose from, and it's up to you to select your best team before each match is played. No two players are alike, and each of them has a different **Skill**. This is a single number which reflects everything about that player's footballing ability: the higher the better. They've all got different personalities, strengths and weaknesses; and certain combinations of footballers play well together. You'll get to meet your players on page 10.

The Other Managers

You are not the only manager trying to win the league this year! Nine other teams are trying to beat you to the top of the table, and you will play each of them in turn. The other managers are introduced on page 24, so keep reading – it's always worth getting to know your enemy . . .

Playing Matches

Each time Saturday comes around, you will play a match against one of your opponents. The rules for playing matches are on page 28. If you like, you can skip them for now and come back to them when it's time to play your first match.

The League Tables

Remember, there are ten teams in the league; so whenever you play a match, everyone else plays one too. Each time you finish a match, you will be told the scores from these other games. Just like in real life, this can change the positions of the teams in the league. If you don't know already, these are the rules for awarding points:

Win: +3 points
Draw: +1 point
Lose: +0 points

At the back of this book is a series of blank League Tables. You fill one in after every game you play, putting the team with the most points at the top. As well as the points won, you should also fill in the number of goals scored for and against each team. This will help you work out the Goal Difference: for example, a team with 9 goals for and 7 goals against has a Goal Difference of +2.

Player Substitutions

At any time during a match, you can substitute a player. There's only one rule: neither team may do this more than three times in any one match. If you substitute a player, it's best to replace him with someone who plays in the same position (eg. a Defender for a Defender). But if you use someone from a different position, you must subtract 2 from that player's Skill for as long as he plays there.

Injuries and Sendings-Off

During matches, players may get injured or sent off and must be removed from the pitch. An injured player may be substituted; a sent-off player may not! Injured players take time to get fit again, and this will depend on your team's Fitness score.

Player Recovery

Before each match, roll one dice for each injured player in your squad. If the number you roll is lower than your team's Fitness, that player has made a full recovery. If it's equal or higher, he's still injured and cannot play in that match!

And Finally . . .

You are now ready to begin your adventure. Solving the mystery and winning the league is not easy! So remember, if you don't succeed the first time through, you can always go back to the beginning and start again as many times as you like.

So now read on – it's time to meet your players.

Player Profiles

Jamie Coates

Skill:	5	Last Season's Stats:	
Position:	Goalkeeper	Goals:	0
Born:	Fife 2/9/70	Yellow Cards:	0
Height:	6ft 3in	Red Cards:	1
Weight:	13st 2lb		

There's no place for daydreaming or crowd-pleasing in the goalmouth. Your goalie is your last line of defence, and what you want is someone solid, quick and reliable with big hands and good vision to stop balls. Here's your man: Jamie's a stalwart who's been with the club longer than anyone. Does exactly what it says on the tin.

JAMIE COATES

Rob Rose

Skill:	5	Last Season's Stats:	
Position:	Goalkeeper	Goals:	1
Born:	Oxford 31/12/81	Yellow Cards:	2
Height:	6ft 1in	Red Cards:	0
Weight:	12st 8lb		

ROB ROSE

Rob has been HCFC's second-choice goalie for a couple of years, and some say he is now mature enough to take the regular position. He's younger and livelier than Jamie, but on a bad day you've seen indecision and hot-headedness let this young man down. Still, he's a dynamic lad who's shown great promise; never more so than when heading in an equaliser off a corner against Bridgford last season. Not bad for a goalie in injury time!

Steve Fitzgerald

Skill:	5		Last Season's Stats:	
Position:	Defender		Goals:	0
Born:	Liverpool 19/9/78		Yellow Cards:	3
Height:	6ft 1in		Red Cards:	0
Weight:	10st 7lb			

Pairs well with: de Carvalho (D)

On dark, wet winter evenings when the rest of your squad wishes they were at home, Steve seems to grow in stature. He's a powerful and gritty full-back who can dig deep when it's needed and fights for every loose ball. Focused and brave, Steve is a real asset to your

STEVE FITZGERALD

team, though some of the more 'stylish' players complain he can be insensitive to their needs on the pitch. Fitzy doesn't care. He's just doing his job.

Joe Fry

		Last Season's Stats:	
Skill:	4		
Position:	Defender	Goals:	0
Born:	Cardiff 2/11/77	Yellow Cards:	4
Height:	5ft 10in	Red Cards:	2
Weight:	11st 6lb		

Pairs well with: Hurley (M)

Despite accusations of being a dirty – some would say X-rated – player, Fry is never one to shy away from a sliding tackle. He might not be the sharpest tool in the shed, but here is a player you can trust to give 110% for the full ninety minutes. Useful.

JOE FRY

Antek Bobak

		Last Season's Stats:	
Skill:	5		
Position:	Defender	Goals:	1
Born:	Krakow 17/6/75	Yellow Cards:	1
Height:	5ft 11in	Red Cards:	1
Weight:	11st 12lb		

Pairs well with: Bostock (M), Hoggart (M)

Polish-born Antek plays a classy game. He's cool-headed deep in defence, but confident enough to run a stray ball up the field and have a pop from thirty yards. He sometimes appears not to hear what you say, and when he's decided on a course of action he'll stubbornly follow it through whatever you shout from the touchline; but this warhorse is a thoughtful and mature full-back with a right hoof guaranteed to find row Z when it matters.

ANTEK BOBAK

Ricky Neville

Skill:	4		Last Season's Stats:	
Position:	Defender		Goals:	0
Born:	London 16/5/79		Yellow Cards:	2
Height:	6ft 0in		Red Cards:	0
Weight:	13st 4lb			

RICKY NEVILLE

Pairs well with: Duval (M)
Sticky Ricky, the fans call him. Mr Neville marks his man like he's glued to him. No messing about on the field here; Ricky once sat down and read Alec Handsome's *Call That Defending?* from cover to cover, and he plays a textbook game to the letter. Off the field it's

a different story, and any bottle this player shows in defence is matched by the bottles he's been known to put away down the Admiral Rodney. Needs a firm hand.

Carlos de Carvalho

Skill:	6	Last Season's Stats:	
Position:	Defender	Goals:	0
Born:	Lisbon 5/8/82	Yellow Cards:	1
Height:	6ft 1in	Red Cards:	1
Weight:	10st 13lb		

CARLOS DE CARVALHO

Pairs well with: Fitzgerald (D)
Your greatest bargain! Carlos came over from Portugal six months ago on a temporary loan and decided to stay. He says he likes the food here. The fans certainly like him, and there's no point in fighting the fashionable flamboyance in players like this. Whether he's scissor-kicking deep crosses or clearing balls off the line with his head, Carlos gives the paying public their money's worth. But he needs to learn to play a team game, and you hope he won't let overzealousness get the better of him.

Will 'Frog' Frost

Skill:	5	**Last Season's Stats:**	
Position:	Midfielder	Goals:	2
Born:	Birmingham 15/4/75	Yellow Cards:	4
Height:	5ft 9in	Red Cards:	0
Weight:	10st 11lb		

Pairs well with: Parker (A)

Will Frost is what you call a play-maker. His weight can count against him as he can be scythed down by the bigger boys, but his low centre of gravity means he can leave his opponents standing with sudden changes of direction and darting runs up the flank. When Frog turns and quick-steps to carve a swathe through the midfield you'd challenge anyone not to call this game beautiful.

WILL 'FROG' FROST

Michael Hurley

Skill:	5	**Last Season's Stats:**	
Position:	Midfielder	Goals:	2
Born:	Cork 9/10/78	Yellow Cards:	3
Height:	6ft 0in	Red Cards:	1
Weight:	11st 8lb		

Pairs well with: Fry (D), Wehnert (M)

Mick is a shy and quiet lad off the pitch, but in a match situation he is a real asset. His workhorse attitude and fluidity of passing mean he's never far from the ball: a team-player in every sense of the word.

MICHAEL HURLEY

Dmitri Duval

Skill: 4
Position: Midfielder
Born: Toulouse 5/6/77
Height: 6ft 1in
Weight: 13st 0lb

Last Season's Stats:
Goals: 1
Yellow Cards: 3
Red Cards: 0

DMITRI DUVAL

Pairs well with: Neville (D)
Duval is a perfectionist. He can be quick to blame his team-mates if they make mistakes in training or if they go to sleep during a match, but he pulls his weight for Hardwick and the squad grudgingly respects him. He has a wealth of experience from playing football in four countries, and plays a neat quick passing game using the full width of the pitch. English football could learn something from this Frenchman.

Anthony Bostock

Skill: 5
Position: Midfielder
Born: Brighton 28/3/80
Height: 6ft 0in
Weight: 11st 9lb

Last Season's Stats:
Goals: 3
Yellow Cards: 2
Red Cards: 1

Pairs well with:
Bobak (D), Stevens (A)
Except when he's turning the team showers to cold, hiding Salvatore's St Christopher or doing impressions of you, Ant Bostock is a bright and loyal player who never gives you any trouble. He's a bit lively for some of the squad's old guard, but his wit makes him good at diffusing bickering within the team. He's even better in a dead-ball situation, and has produced some masterful free kicks and corners in his time. Can he kick it? Yes he can.

ANTHONY BOSTOCK

Klaus 'The General' Wehnert

Skill: 6
Position: Midfielder
Born: Stuttgart 18/11/76
Height: 6ft 4in
Weight: 13st 12lb

Last Season's Stats:
Goals: 1
Yellow Cards: 1
Red Cards: 0

KLAUS 'THE GENERAL' WEHNERT

Pairs well with:
Hurley (M), Leslie (A)
This brute of a central midfielder has been known to win balls by sheer intimidation. They don't come much bigger than German-born Klaus, but although a little sluggish his passing is clinical and he is surprisingly deft on the ball. He is unselfish and cooperative on the field, preferring link-up play to displays of individual prowess. Good vision and natural leadership make Wehnert a lynchpin for your midfield unit.

John 'Larry' Hoggart

Skill:	4		
Position:	Midfielder		
Born:	Tasmania 1/7/79		
Height:	6ft 1in		
Weight:	11st 9lb		

Last Season's Stats:
Goals: 1
Yellow Cards: 2
Red Cards: 1

Pairs well with:
Bobak (D), Wood (A)
John Hoggart's critics have suggested that if he ever gives up football, he could have a second career in acting. Admittedly, you'd think he's broken every bone in his body when he goes

JOHN 'LARRY' HOGGART

over following a tackle; but his after-goal backflips are equally OTT and he keeps Hardwick energised as well as he winds up the opposition. This Aussie is serious about his football though, and with sure control and quick dribbling runs he brings real flair and excitement to the game.

Ian Leslie

Skill:	5	Last Season's Stats:	
Position:	Attacker	Goals:	4
Born:	London 10/2/79	Yellow Cards:	1
Height:	5ft 6in	Red Cards:	0
Weight:	10st 5lb		

Pairs well with: Wehnert (M)
Being of less-than-average height for a footballer means Ian isn't your first choice to be on the receiving end of a cross in the box, right? Wrong. This little guy is all muscle and somehow he gets his head on the end of high crosses by sheer speed and timing. More than once you've seen Leslie lose his nerve under pressure, and he is something of a recluse in the footballing arena

IAN LESLIE

as he's never given a single interview. But for as long as he's knocking those floaters into the back of the onion bag, you've got no complaints.

Jed Stevens

		Last Season's Stats:	
Skill:	5		
Position:	Attacker	Goals:	6
Born:	London 7/7/78	Yellow Cards:	1
Height:	6ft 1in	Red Cards:	1
Weight:	13st 8lb		

Pairs well with: Bostock (M)

JED STEVENS

No one knows how they do it, but some strikers just have a knack of being in the right place at the right time. Here's one of them. You once brought Jed on as a sub in the seventy-fifth minute, and by the eightieth he'd turned a one-nil deficit into a two-one lead. He says it's because his dad used to take him poaching as a kid, and he's learned to take his chances. This might also explain his inclination to hang around lazily waiting for crosses; but if someone's feeding them, Stevens is putting them away.

Toby Wood

		Last Season's Stats:	
Skill:	6		
Position:	Attacker	Goals:	5
Born:	Nottingham 16/9/77	Yellow Cards:	2
Height:	5ft 10in	Red Cards:	0
Weight:	12st 8lb		

TOBY WOOD

Pairs well with: Hoggart (M)
One of Toby's strengths is the set piece. His combination of tactical analysis and a cultured left foot can undo the tightest back line, and he is quick to punish defensive errors. He's not your Sunday league type who tirelessly presses forward to wear down the defence, and he can appear to lose interest in a stalemate; but if his team-mates are on form and accurate, Woody can work the scoring zone as though he owned it. Goalkeepers beware.

Ben Parker

Skill:	5	Last Season's Stats:	
Position:	Attacker	Goals:	8
Born:	Harrogate 1/3/86	Yellow Cards:	2
Height:	5ft 11in	Red Cards:	2
Weight:	11st 2lb		

Pairs well with:
Frost (M), Duce (A)
What this lad doesn't know about football isn't worth knowing. The youngest player in your squad, Ben is also one of the brightest. His ability to turn on the ball and think on his feet make him a

BEN PARKER

lethal striker and exciting to watch, but his youth means he can be impetuous.

Salvatore 'The Duke' Duce

Skill: 4
Position: Attacker
Born: Florence 12/12/72
Height: 6ft 1in
Weight: 10st 7lb

Last Season's Stats:
Goals: 5
Yellow Cards: 4
Red Cards: 0

SALVATORE 'THE DUKE' DUCE

Pairs well with: Parker (A)
The papers call him vain and a show-off, but the fans and the ladies love Salvatore. His deadly accurate right-foot and natural Italian flamboyance make The Duke ideal in this goal-scoring role, and he's consistently the best penalty-taker in your squad. He does have a tendency to get homesick though, especially after he's been on the phone to his mother.

Danny Knox

Skill:	8	Last Season's Stats:	
Position:	Attacker	Goals:	15
Born:	London 15/8/80	Yellow Cards:	2
Height:	6ft 0in	Red Cards:	0
Weight:	11st 8lb		

Hardwick's hero and team captain. What more can be said? Danny averaged almost a goal a game last season, and the whole squad look up to him for strength and inspiration. He's hard-working, reliable, fair and, most importantly, committed to this club. Whatever would you do without him?

DANNY KNOX

Manager Profiles

Dave Curtis
Bridgford City

Dave Curtis has had a rocky relationship with the fans ever since taking his role as player-manager. He has led Bridgford City to some modest league successes but has made some unpopular decisions along the way.

Quote: 'Football's all about tough choices. If you can't stand the heat, get out of the dressing room.'

DAVE CURTIS

HARRY SHAW

Harry Shaw
Epperstone Town

Sometimes a manager comes along who just strikes a chord. Five years in the job and no major trophies; but the fans and the players love Harry Shaw for his friendly, informal system of management. Quote: 'My players are my sons. I believe in the carrot and not the stick.'

Jules Torrence
Gonalston City

A big cash injection from the new owner has given long-time manager Jules Torrence

JULES TORRENCE

new hope. If he fails to bring league success to Gonalston this season, his fans will be less than forgiving.

Quote: 'With my new signings, no one's going to get in our way this time.'

JAKE TAPPER

Jake Tapper
Gunthorpe United

Jake Tapper has attracted criticism from the press with his evangelical approach to football. But his charisma is winning the hearts and minds of his team, and he sees success as his destiny this season. His style of management contrasts starkly with that of rival Bill Drebble, whose blood boils at everything Jake says.

Quote: 'God loves this club. Through me, His work will be done this season.'

Bill Drebble
Lowdham Athletic

Bill is a lifelong Athletic fan and is well-respected at the club for his no-nonsense style. But he is renowned for having a fiery temper, and his hostility towards Jake Tapper, manager of rival club Gunthorpe United, is legendary.

BILL DREBBLE

Quote: 'If we beat Gunthorpe ten-nil and lost every other match this season, I'd still be happy.'

ERIC REDMAN

Eric Redman
Lambley Rovers

Eric is one of the old guard: he's managed fifteen teams in four different countries during a distinguished career. He's been brought in at great expense for his first season with strugglers Lambley Rovers, and the fans hope he'll bring vital experience to the club.

Quote: 'Football's the same all over the world. Wherever I lay my sheepskin coat, that's my home.'

Jack Tatchell
Oxton Wanderers

Jack has a reputation for a hard-nosed approach to management. His critics call him secretive and a bully. His admirers say he knows what he wants and gets results.

Quote: 'Judge me not on what you read. Judge me on what I achieve.'

JACK TATCHELL

SAM SHAUGHNESSY

Sam Shaughnessy
Papplewick Town

Sam Shaughnessy is a young, ambitious manager who has risen through the ranks from his early days as youth player at the club. Well-known, respected and dedicated to his team.

Quote: 'This club is my world. I live and die by Papplewick.'

José Torrego
Woodborough County

When he played for Spain as a centre-forward, José Torrego was capped 56 times. He's now making a serious bid for management success at English club level.

Quote: 'España es mi mujer. Woodborough es mi amante. Amo a las dos.'

JOSÉ TORREGO

VICTOR

Your Club Chairman
Victor Sinkowski

Victor is your boss – a wealthy businessman for whom success and money come before football. He keeps a close eye on how the club is run, but takes a back seat in all footballing decisions. Victor's clever investments and financial expertise have helped make Hardwick City wealthy, but you sometimes wonder if he even knows what offside means . . . Still, he holds all the cards when it comes to the club's finances and is certainly not a man to cross.

Rules of Matchplay

Here are the rules for playing each of your matches. It's a bit like match highlights – as you go along, you will see the important events of the match unfold. The rules are really easy once you get used to them, and there's an example at the end to help you.

1. Start with a fresh Match Sheet. You'll find these starting on page 206.

2. Pick your team. First you'll need a Goalkeeper. Then you'll need 10 other players. These can be any combination you like of Defence, Midfield and Attack; but you must choose at least two of each. You'll probably want to pick the ones with the highest Skill scores, but you should also keep an eye on who plays well together (you'll find this information in Player Profiles on page 10). Remember: you can't use a player if he is injured, or if he was sent off in the last game.

3. Write the names and Skills of your chosen players on the Match Sheet.

4. Add up the Skills of all the players in your team (use a calculator if you like). This is your Overall Skill. You'll be told what your opponent's Overall Skill is each time you play a match.

5. Put these numbers in the boxes below. Fill in the Morale

and Fitness scores for your team as well. You should already have made a note of these on your Fact Sheet. Finally, work out the Match Factor at the end of the row. The higher your Match Factor, the better your chance of winning.

6. You're now ready for play to begin! You play a match by rolling dice. If your Match Factor is higher than zero, add 1 to your dice rolls. If it's lower, you must subtract 1 from your dice rolls.

Now look at the table below:

Your roll	Event
4 or less	They score!
5	Special
6, 7 or 8	Time + 1
9	Special
10 or more	You score!

A football match is divided into six sections of 15 minutes each, and these are shown on the 'Referee's Watch' section of your Match Sheet. Whenever you roll a 6, 7 or 8, you'll see the table above says Time + 1. That means 15 minutes have gone by – cross off the number '15' on the ref's watch. Each time you get Time + 1, cross off the next number. When you've crossed off the number '90' the match is over.

You'll also see that if you get a 5 or a 9, a Special Event happens. That means you must now roll two dice again (**don't add**

or subtract anything this time) and consult the Special Event table:

Your roll	Special Event
2	Penalty to them
3	Injury – your player
4	Card – your player
5	Free kick to them
6	Corner to them
7	Time + 1
8	Corner to you
9	Free kick to you
10	Card – their player
11	Injury – their player
12	Penalty to you

⚽ If it's a Penalty, roll one dice. 3, 4, 5 or 6 = Goal!

⚽ If it's a Free kick, roll one dice. 5 or 6 = Goal!

⚽ If it's a Corner, roll one dice. 6 = Goal!

⚽ If one of your players is injured, roll two dice – the number you roll is the number of the injured player. You can substitute him if you want. This might change your Overall Skill. Remember you may only make three substitutions in each game.

⚽ If a player is shown a card, roll one dice. If you roll 1, 2 or 3, the card is red: he is sent off! You're not allowed to substitute him this time, so cross him off your Match Sheet. Remember this will also reduce your Overall Skill. A 4, 5 or 6 means a yellow card – but if that same player is shown two yellow cards in a match, he is sent off. You find out which player has been shown a card in the same way as with injuries.

⚽ If one of their players is injured, their Overall Skill drops by 2 points. If one of their players is sent off, their Overall Skill drops by 5 points.

Remember that if Overall Skill changes, your Match Factor will change as well.

Here's an example to help you:

⚽ Your Overall Skill score is 60. Lowdham Athletic's Overall Skill is 66. You have a Morale and Fitness of 4 each and your Home Advantage gives you +3 in this match. So your Match Factor is $60 - 66 + 4 + 4 + 3 = 5$. This is more than zero, so you can add 1 to your dice rolls.

⚽ Your first roll is 7, add 1 makes 8. Time + 1. Cross off the number 15 on the ref's watch.

⚽ Your second roll is 9, add 1 makes 10. You score! Write the score on your Match Sheet, and the name of the scorer (you choose).

⚽ Your third roll is 4, add 1 makes 5. Special Event: roll two dice. You roll a 3 – one of your players has been injured! You roll two dice to see which one, and you roll 9 – you look on your Match Sheet and it's Klaus Wehnert this time. He had a Skill of 6 and your best substitute Midfielder is Will Frost (Skill

5). So that means your Match Factor is down by 1; but it's still above zero, so you can keep adding 1 to your dice rolls.

⚽ Your fourth roll is 5, add 1 makes 6. Time + 1 again. Cross off the number 30.

⚽ Your fifth roll is 8, add 1 makes 9. Special Event again: roll two dice. You roll a 5 – free kick to them. Roll one dice to see what happens – you roll a 6. They've scored! Write the score on your Match Sheet.

⚽ Your sixth roll is 6, add 1 makes 7. Cross off 45 on the ref's watch. That means it's half-time, and the score is one-all.

You play the second half in exactly the same way – and that's all there is to it! Whenever you win a match, add 1 to your Morale because of the feel-good factor. Whenever you lose a match, you lose 1 Morale.

Let The Game Begin!

If there is a record for gum-chewing or nail-biting, you broke it today . . .

Standing with your coaching staff in the dugout, you hold your breath and wince as a shot whizzes just wide of the post and sails into the crowd.

You can't remember the last time a game was as tense as this; Leslie had put you in the lead in the 34th minute with a pinpoint header off a corner, but some 'enthusiastic' defending from Fry in the box had given Borfield Albion a penalty just after the break. Their striker had coolly dispatched it to the noisy delight of the home fans, and it's still 1-1 in the 85th minute.

You can feel the tension in the visitors' stand behind you – three thousand of your loyal fans willing Hardwick City on. Borfield are in possession in their own half. A neat passing movement beats Hurley in the central midfield, and then a lofted ball finds their man on the right flank.

'Come on, close him down,' you say to yourself through gritted teeth.

But Borfield are moving well and your defence is beaten as the ball falls to their striker who takes it on the half-volley. The ball starts to dip and is flying towards the top left corner of your goal – but Coates jumps high and takes a lightning save! The home fans let out a groan. The referee is looking at his watch – surely that's got to be the last chance?

'Just blow the whistle,' you think as Coates quickly throws the ball out to Neville, who takes it on the run. A short pass to Duval on the left wing, who flicks it over the heads of the midfield right into the path of your top striker, Danny Knox! Borfield over-stretched themselves in that last attack, and they're wide open at the back as Knox surges forward. Just one defender to beat . . .

Your fans are up on their feet and there's a deathly hush in the dugout as Knox reaches the eighteen-yard line. He makes to go left, but then dummies and hops neatly over the outstretched boot of the defender, before unleashing a ferocious right-footed shot straight through the keeper's legs and into the back of the net.

That was the last of the pre-season qualifiers and had seen Hardwick City FC through to the Premier Mini-League. Four years in the job here at the club and you never get bored of the rush of winning. Back home, you went over the 2-1 victory in your mind as the triumphant songs of the fans echoed in your ears.

'He wears red socks
He's a danger in the box
Danny Knox, Danny Knox'

Knox had been mobbed by the other players after his spectacu-lar goal, and everyone had gone home tired and happy. With Danny hitting the top of his form and the squad working well as a unit, you reckon the team could be in with a real chance of tak-ing the title this season.

Then the phone rings, bringing the news which will change your life for ever.

'Good evening. This is Detective Chief Inspector Higson. I'm afraid we have a matter of the utmost gravity which requires your immediate cooperation.'

'What's going on?'

'I'm very sorry, but we need you at the station immediately.'

You get straight into your car and drive the ten minutes to the police station. When you arrive, DCI Higson ushers you silently into a bare, grey-walled interview room.

'Are you going to tell me what's going on?' you ask as he clicks the door shut.

'At 9 o'clock this evening,' he begins grimly, 'one of our patrols reported an abandoned car. It had been forced off the road into a ditch, the driver's window had been smashed, and there was evidence of a struggle. We've traced the registration plate, and the vehicle has been confirmed as belonging to an employee of yours. A Mr Daniel Knox.'

Your skin prickles as the words sink in.

'Maybe he had an accident,' you suggest desperately. 'Have you tried calling him at home?'

'Of course,' the Inspector replies. 'His wife answered. He never arrived home. We're treating this as a kidnap.'

Your mind races, and your first thoughts are with Danny's wife and how awful this must be for her. You struggle with what to say. 'I – I can't believe this. Where is he? Who's taken him?'

The Inspector stares at you with pale grey eyes. 'I'd rather hoped you could tell me.'

Two challenges lie ahead: you must steer Hardwick City to the top of the league, while doing everything in your power to find Danny Knox and bring his assailants to justice. As you progress through the book you will play out each of Hardwick's fixtures in the league, carefully selecting your team each week and using your five million pound budget to build the best squad you can. At the same time, you must use every ounce of your intelligence and cunning to piece together the clues that might just bring your team's best asset back alive . . . Do you have what it takes to do both?

**Now it's time to become the
Big Match Manager!**

1

Friday 14th

You are in your office at Hardwick City Football Club. It's 10:30pm, nearly a week now since Danny Knox disappeared, and the police are no closer to finding him. 'We're doing our best,' is all DCI Higson could tell you, but you know there's almost no chance of getting him safely back in time for tomorrow's match against Lowdham Athletic.

You grab your coat and briefcase, ready to leave for the night. But as you open your office door, you are startled by the desk phone ringing. So late at night . . . Do you go back and answer it (turn to 373), or listen carefully while the answering machine picks it up (turn to 403)?

2

No one else seems to agree that today's result was particularly good for a home game. Lose **2** Morale points after your gaffe, and turn to 104.

3

Are urgent letters ever good news? Sure enough, it's a letter from your team sponsors telling you they are pulling out of their contract 'because of all the bad publicity surrounding Mr Knox'. How dare they – of all the selfish things to do! This could mean financial ruin for the club, unless you can broker a new deal soon. Two other local companies expressed recent interest in getting their logos on the Hardwick strip, and a phone call to one of them could do it. But which is the right choice?

SureTech Phones   (Turn to 261)
Topflight Sportswear   (Turn to 369)

4

There is a muffled crack and Danny is knocked backwards over his chair. He lies motionless, blood from the wound in his temple making a dark stain on your carpet. Your last thought is how annoyed the office cleaner will be in the morning. Then Victor squeezes the trigger for the second time this evening.

Turn to 101.

5

'What's up then, you two? Don't think I haven't noticed.'
They glare at each other.
'He's been after my job since he got here,' spits Ricky.

'Reckons he's all that.'

'Yeah, whatever, big man. If you were any good you'd prove it,' retorts Jonny provocatively, squaring up to him.

They're acting like a couple of macho schoolboys. How pathetic – do you leave them to get on with it (turn to 385) or intervene (turn to 301)?

6

Monday comes to an end, and your team has worked hard for you. You could really make their day something to remember here. Do you have champagne you'd like to treat them to? If so, turn to 210. If you'd rather not, turn to 48.

7

You pull open the door to the cupboard, revealing the steel door of a safe. It's set fast in the concrete of the garage wall, and looks very heavy. No wonder Victor didn't bother to lock the garage. There is a small keyhole in the right of the door, and in the middle is a combination wheel surrounded by numbers. Do you have a combination you would like to try? If so, it will be made up of three numbers. Add those numbers together and turn to that paragraph. If not, there's no point guessing – there are a million possible combinations! Leave well alone and get back to your office by turning to 392.

8

The body of a young woman is hanging by the neck from the light fitting in the centre of the room. Her hands are tied behind her back and you can't see her face as her head has been covered with a pillowcase. The room is a mess: all the drawers have been emptied on to the bed, and the power pack for her laptop has been wrenched out of the wall. The laptop has gone.

Pull yourself together! What are you going to do?

To search the room for clues, turn to 242.

To take down the corpse, turn to 220.

To leave as quickly as possible, turn to 30.

9

You let the door click quietly shut behind you, and you find your-self standing alone in the spacious opulence of Victor's office. You cast a curious eye over the expensive furnishings. Directly behind his desk hang the framed certificates of his corporate

successes. On the wall facing you is a trio of oil paintings depicting ruddy-faced country gentlemen on rain-soaked moors, rifles cocked over-arm and sleek dogs carrying limp game-birds in wet jaws. Covering most of the wall to your right is a heavy oak cabinet lined with business manuals in leather-bound volumes – the kind that smell nice – and next to that is a long, creamy low-backed sofa. What do you have in mind? Would you rather search the desk (turn to 81), examine the cabinet (turn to 303) or leave immediately (turn to 398)?

10

'Nice attitude,' you tell him, and leave. Is money all anyone cares about these days? You may visit one of the other establishments if you wish. If so turn back to 200 and study the picture. Otherwise you may drive back home by turning to 358.

11

The whistle to signal start of play is accompanied by the usual rise in volume from the huge body of support that has turned up for this fixture. In the first five minutes it is clear that the Bridgford defence is particularly shaky, and the attacks are all coming from your side. Add up the Skills of your Attackers. Is your total:

  12 or less?   (Turn to 214)
  More than 12?   (Turn to 124)

12

Ian is on his way out to the training pitch to practise ball skills.

'You're in early,' you comment as he passes you in the corridor.

'I'm committed to this team,' he tells you. 'I want to make sure I'm a permanent fixture.'

How nice to have players with such enthusiasm. Turn to 352.

13

You stride across the car park and take the steps two at a time. You enter the club buildings through the revolving door just as Victor appears, hurrying in the opposite direction. He doesn't seem to have seen you and you watch as he heaves himself inside his car. If you decide to follow him, turn to 441. If you take this opportunity to search his office again, turn to 43. If you'd prefer to leave well alone, turn to 281.

14

You are standing in the admin office where the secretaries work, but as it's Saturday it's deserted. Facing you are three large desks and a shelf full of files. Do you wish to search further? If so, turn to 457. If not, go back to your room plan at 107 and decide where to go next.

15

Is this a one-horse race or what? There's no stopping you, and you are announced as this month's top manager! Does it ever get boring being this good? Thought not. Add **3** Morale for your impressive 100% record, and when you've stopped looking at yourself in the mirror you may turn to 347.

16

'There's still time to nail this match,' you think to yourself as you pop another stick of gum in your mouth. It's been a tiring game, but you are impressed with your men as they push forward yet again. Some calm, confident passing in the midfield opens up a gap down the right flank, and your No. 7 shirt is able to make a run into their danger zone. He is charged down by their left-back, but not before he whips a lofted ball into the box and the referee plays the advantage. And just as you'd practised, you have a man making a run in at the far post. You are on your feet now, and you have a perfect view as he is body-checked by a beefy Papplewick defender and goes sprawling to the floor.

'PENALTY!!' you scream at the top of your voice. And the man in black agrees with you. It certainly is a funny old game – but there's nothing the Papplewick men can do about that as they surround the ref in protest, who shoos them away like flies and calmly points to the spot.

Choose now who you want to take the spot-kick, gather your dice and turn to 328.

17

'Who's there?' you demand in a slightly shaky voice.

Your heart sinks as Victor enters the room. He stops abruptly when he sees you. But his startled expression soon changes to a sly grin.

'Well, this rather makes things easier, wouldn't you say?'

He is still smiling as he takes a step towards you.

'I've been looking for an excuse to get rid of you for a few weeks now. And now I've caught you stealing from my office, I think you've given me one.'

You know there's no use in protesting, and you let your shoulders slump.

'I accept your resignation,' he snarls threateningly. 'Now get out.'

Turn to 101.

18

Check your Match Sheet. Are Anthony Bostock and Jed Stevens both playing in the match at this moment? If so turn to 212. If not, turn to 256.

19

You press the clutch and pull on the handbrake as you sit wondering which road to take. It has started to rain, and this part of Oxton is deserted. It seems. Because a hundred yards behind you, the black saloon is accelerating. For the last half-mile it has been crawling behind you with lights off, and it is almost invisible in the gloom. You are blinded temporarily when two headlights suddenly blaze like suns in your rear-view mirror before the saloon smashes into the back of your car, throwing you forward and stalling the engine. Your head is ringing with the impact; only your seatbelt saved your brain from being splattered all over the dashboard. And as you blink the confusion from your eyes, you see that each wing mirror is reflecting a man walking towards you and carrying a gun. What will you do? Try to start the engine (turn to 166)? Or get out of the car to confront them (turn to 182)?

20

Turn to 154.

21

Luckily for you, the driver in front seems to have urgent business to attend to, and you are just able to clear the lights. Turn to 188.

22

You try the handle but the door is locked. The time you've wasted means this counts as one of your six rooms, I'm afraid. What are you expecting to find, anyway? Go back to your room plan on 107 and try somewhere else.

23

As the training week progresses, you watch as your defensive unit really tightens up. Your focus on defence should really pay off in an away fixture. For the next match only, add **1** to the Skill of any two of your Defenders. Now turn to 34.

24

Oh. My. God. Your team has never had so much respect for you. Wherever you learnt to speak like that it paid off in the dressing room today. Gain **2** Morale, and add **1** to the Skill of any three of your players for the next match only. Has there been a recent falling-out between two players in your squad? If so, turn to 325. Otherwise, with chest out and head held high, turn to 34.

25

Terrified of Victor returning, you begin to search swiftly and quietly. On his desk is a pot of pens, and at the bottom of the pot is a small brass key, marked with the number 152. Take the key and make a note of its number on your Fact Sheet. When you've put everything back where you found it you can pack up and leave for the day – turn to 398.

26

Your striker is sitting in the dressing room with a glum expression on his face.

'Morning, Ian! You're in early.'

'I'm not happy here, boss,' he tells you, without looking up. 'I didn't come here to play reserve matches every week. I know I'm under contract but I'd like to leave.'

It's one of the hardest things about being a manager. How do you keep a whole squad of professionals happy when you can only play eleven of them in each match? Sometimes the ambitious ones will get restless if you don't make them feel wanted. You must subtract **2** from Ian's Skill in every match from now on until another club offers to buy him.

Turn to 352.

27

You push into first and edge forward as the traffic begins to move. The narrow road begins to widen, feeding two lanes of traffic together. To be sure you never lose sight of Victor ahead you try to make ground by switching lane, but in doing so you cut up a man in a white van who slams on his horn and shows you his favourite finger. You grip the steering wheel and hope you haven't drawn attention to yourself. Roll one dice. If you roll 1, turn to 188. If you roll 2–6 turn to 67.

28

You follow the oil spill but it stops a little way down the road. You drive in circles for a while but there's no trace of him. Do you go back and search the phonebox (turn to 149) or go home for the night (turn to 300)?

29

Viv motions for you to stand to one side as you approach the door. He knocks rapidly three times.

'Who is it?' asks a suspicious voice from inside.

'Mother Hen,' Viv says confidently. He looks at you and puts a finger to his lips.

The door is opened from the inside, and the guard hardly knows what's hit him as Viv brings the side of his hand swiftly down on to the side of his thick neck. The guard's legs crumple and he falls to the floor, and you see the treasure he was guarding. A young man of about twenty-five is sitting on a chair in the middle of the room, his mouth and hands bound with nylon ropes. His eyes flash when he recognises you and he strains to get up.

'Danny – thank God – come on, it's OK, you're coming home.'

Viv pulls a knife from his boot and cuts the bonds from Danny's face and hands. He rubs his wrists and looks at you.

'Jesus, boss. You took your time.'

Viv helps you get Danny up and outside to the car. He is thinner than before but he still has those bright eyes and resolute expression you remember from the day you hired him.

'Let's go, Viv,' you hurry, climbing in the driver's side and clicking your seatbelt.

'No. You two go. The other guy won't be far behind, and I want to make sure he gets a nice surprise.' Turn to 378.

30

You run out of the room, down the corridor, and straight into two detectives at the top of the stairs. Close behind them are four armed officers. You are quickly overpowered and taken away for questioning. Turn to 433.

31

Hoggart cuts in from the right and the two have the Gunthorpe defender in a pincer. He stands his ground to head off John Hoggart, but your midfielder has his wits about him. A perfectly well-timed pass sees the ball at the feet of Toby Wood who is in the box with only the keeper to beat. Woody's been here a million times before – like every night when he falls asleep – and he wastes no time in drilling the ball past the shipwrecked keeper and into the waiting goal. Turn to 366.

32

Congratulations! You are announced as this month's top manager! It was a close call, but with your impressive goal difference and disciplinary record you were the obvious choice. Carry on like this and you'll win the league for sure. Add **2** Morale for your achievement and turn to 347.

33

Their goalie has been left stranded by Stevens and Bostock's neat manoeuvre, and can't get across in time to stop the ball hitting the underside of the crossbar . . . and dropping behind the line! A well-deserved goal from a finely-tuned set piece, and you leap from your chair to applaud your players as they celebrate in front of the ecstatic supporters. Now carry on with the rest of the match, a goal to the good – and turn to 377 when it's all over.

34

Friday 18th
It's the day before your next away fixture. You don't want to risk injuring any of your players, so you instruct your training staff to give them a day of light fitness work and a long warm-down. While they're working, you spend the afternoon in your office catching up with the latest moves in the transfer markets and getting some paperwork out of the way. Your phone rings and you answer absent-mindedly, assuming it's your secretary telling you the players have finished.

It's not. Turn to 436.

35

This week's training session is a mess! Your attackers can't find the crosses, your goalies fumble every ball, and the midfielders are falling over each other. Sometimes even the best managers can't perform miracles. Lose **1** Morale, and subtract **1** from the Skill of three of your players for this game only (you choose which ones). Turn to 421.

36

If you haven't done so already, you may take a look at the brown paper parcel (turn to 316), open the letter marked URGENT (turn to 3), or the letter from the FA (turn to 394). If you would rather go and discuss match tactics with your players, turn to 89.

37

How did you get on in your game against Lowdham Athletic?
    If you drew, turn to 410.
    If you beat them, turn to 32.

38

Who do you intend to praise?
    Ricky Neville?   (Turn to 170)
    Klaus Wehnert?   (Turn to 458)
    Jed Stevens?   (Turn to 427)
    No one in particular?   (Turn to 279)

39

You are in the trophy room, a small windowless cabin smelling of polish and dust. Facing you all along one wall is a glass-fronted shelf, which is locked. There 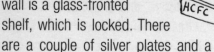 are a couple of silver plates and a Fair Play award, but no major titles. Could you be the one to change all that? When you've finished dreaming, go back to 107 and the room plan.

40

Any advantage you have is being cancelled out by the strength of the opposition in the midfield. If your Match Factor is above zero, you may not add 1 to any more dice rolls until you bring on a substitute Midfielder to replace an Attacker or a Defender. You may do that now if you wish. Then turn to 45.

41

The ball's got wings this time and it's always rising. You and twenty thousand others watch as it flies a foot or so over the crossbar. The goalie looks shaken, though, and you've a feeling this match has more to offer. Turn to 396.

42

Right place, wrong town. You must have missed something. You've had a wasted journey and must now return home. Turn to 358.

43

You stride silently past your office door and creep up the stairs to the executive floor. Why do you always feel like a naughty school-child when you're up here? The plush landing is deserted – the execs must be out massaging each other's egos on the golf course. But there's the door, and there's the shiny brass plate: *Victor Sinkowski*. You try the handle – but of course it's locked. Do you have a key? If you do and you wish to try it in the lock, turn to 353. If you'd prefer to race back and try to pursue Victor, turn to 441. Otherwise turn to 281 to return to your office and get on with your proper job.

44

Your chosen player has responded well in training. For the rest of the season, whenever the opposing team scores a goal, roll two dice. If you roll 11 or 12, treat the shot as offside. Make a note of this on your Fact Sheet next to this Defender's name (it only applies if he is playing). Remember: you can focus on two skills this week. If this was your first, turn back to 351 to choose again from the list. If you have now chosen two, turn to 430.

45

Continue with the match. When 90 minutes are up, turn to 239.

46

Turn to 165.

47

For the next match only, add **1** to the Skill of any two of your Midfielders. Now turn to 6.

48

Saturday 5th
It's the day of your away match against Gonalston City, and you spend the early morning selecting your team. When you've done that, turn to 423.

49

You need to pay closer attention to the headlines! SureTech are in serious financial difficulty, and the deal you struck is not going to bring in enough money this season. Subtract 3 million from your Budget. If this takes your Budget below zero, turn to **444**. If not, curse your financial mismanagement and turn to **139**.

50

The match begins at a furious pace, with tackles flying in all over the place as both teams bid for early domination of the field. Your midfielders are doing a good job of keeping possession, but Lambley look increasingly dangerous as they make forward darting runs into Hardwick territory. Can your back line cope with the onslaught? Add up the Skills of all of your Defenders. Is your total:

Less than 15?	(Turn to 271)
15 or more?	(Turn to 304)

51

'Something wrong, lads?' you ask, twisting round in your seat.

'Nothing, chief,' Will says quickly.

The players look at each other.

'You've got to,' Ian hisses at Will.

'It's just – I've been getting these phone calls at home,' Will begins nervously. 'About four of them now, in the night mostly. This muffled voice, telling me to play badly. Last time he said Danny was first, and I could be next.'

'It's probably just some idiot Gonalston fan, been reading too much about Danny in the paper and decided to put the wind up you,' you reassure him. You insist that no one else at the club is in any danger, but that you will inform the police. You're not convinced though, and you decide to take the precaution of hiring extra security staff just in case.

'Any word on Danny?' asks Ian Leslie hopefully.

'The police say they're getting closer,' you lie. In truth, you know the police are even more stumped than you are.

Turn to 103.

52

Is Michael Hurley a strong presence in your squad, or would you rather have your grandma playing the midfield? See how much you can get for Hurley by rolling one dice and subtracting the number from his Skill. This is how much is being offered in millions. If you'd like to give Mick the flick, take the money and pack his bags. Remember to remove his name from your Fact Sheet and add the money to your Budget.

If the number you got was zero or less, it means no one is interested in buying him at the moment. You can only do this once: when you're ready turn to 454.

53

You walk over to the bar and order a drink. The room is crowded with Gunthorpe fans celebrating their team's victory this afternoon, and a cheer goes up from behind you as the fruit machine noisily chugs out a pile of coins. There is a man sitting at the bar, and you strike up a conversation with him by asking if he's seen anything suspicious recently. He starts telling you about all kinds of secret meetings that have been going on, and has a never-ending supply of stories about Russian spies and aliens. You soon realise he's just a drunk, but each time you try to go he grabs your arm and whispers more secrets to you. By the time you get away everything else has closed. Better drive home – turn to 358.

54

'Beautiful morning, chief!' Rob Rose greets you cheerfully.

'Boss.' Ian Leslie is more reserved, but that's just him.

The players all file on to the bus, and when the kit bags have been stowed, you board and begin the two-hour commute to Gunthorpe. On the way you study the form of the opposition.

Gunthorpe United FC
Overall Skill: 64

Gunthorpe have won three out of five this season, and with Jake Tapper preaching from the front the team is in fearless mood. But technically they are an average side, and if your players keep their heads and combine well together, the better team should win on the day.

Select your team, then turn to 173.

55

You're ready to play. Refer to the rules on page 28, and play out the first half of the match! When you reach half-time, turn to 278.

56

Unluckily for you, Rob dives to the right while the striker sends the ball spinning towards the left of the now open goalmouth. It's a keen shot, but it's curving . . . Roll one dice. If you roll a 6, turn to 197. On 1–5, turn to 379.

57

The Hardwick fans are on their feet applauding the move as the referee waves play on, and you notice that Duval can't keep in a little smile as he runs back to position. Their man is still down, and you've got the advantage – you may add **1** to your next dice roll because of this. Now turn to 80.

58

Which goalie are you using? If it's Jamie Coates, turn to 357. If Rob Rose is your keeper, turn to 56. If you're using a defender, turn to 379.

59

'It's an away game and I want to keep a clean sheet if we can,' you instruct your squad. 'You, you and you' – you point to your defenders – 'I want you closing them down every ball. And you lot' – here you indicate your forwards – 'fall back in a supporting role, and be ready for the long passes when they come.' Your players nod in agreement. How will they respond in training? Roll one dice.

If you roll 1 or 2, turn to 322.
If you roll 3 or 4, turn to 362.
If you roll 5 or 6, turn to 298.

60

Half-time over and the fans are back at their seats with pies and cups of tea. Your midfielders are in position around the centre circle, and they begin pass-

ing the ball around in your half of the field. Within seconds, a poorly-timed pass back to your goalkeeper leaves the ball dangerously unattended and it is charged down by a Bridgford centre-forward. Are you playing the combination of Neville and Duval? If so, turn to 317. If not, turn to 113.

61

If your team won, turn to 195.
If you lost, turn to 343.
If the result was a draw, turn to 121.

62

There's nothing here. Do you stubbornly continue searching under the mat (turn to 96), smash a window (turn to 247) or try the garage door (turn to 187)?

63

Will Frost will play this next match with a Skill **2** points lower than usual. Ian Leslie plays with a Skill **1** point lower. But you don't notice this until half-time, so you may not substitute either player until then. Now turn to 103.

64

Is your defender Steve Fitzgerald on the field? If so, turn to 123. If not, turn to 129.

65

The Papplewick midfield is much stronger than you'd expected today. Wherever your players put the ball, there always seems to be a winger or centre-half ready with a tackle. Add up the Skills of your Midfielders. Is your total:

15 or less?	(Turn to 389)
16–20?	(Turn to 40)
21 or more?	(Turn to 438)

66

You wade in and start throwing your weight around. 'No one talks to my team like that!' you shout, pushing aside a burly Oxton centre-forward. But the more you shout and shove, the more violent the situation becomes. And, worse still, you've been caught on camera and you'll be given a two-match ban from the touch-

line! Very bad move. What were you thinking, encouraging them like that? Roll two dice and take the difference between them. This is the number of players that have been injured from your team and must now be substituted. Now do the same for your opponents. Remember neither side may make more than three substitutions.

Lose **2** Morale as you won't be able to offer support from the bench now. Calm yourself during the interval, then resume the match. When you hear the full-time whistle, turn to 61.

67

You're gaining on Victor's car now and he's in the nearside lane, only just ahead. But without warning he pulls away abruptly down a narrow side street, and as the momentum of the traffic takes you forward you know you've lost him. You curse as you sail past and arrive at a roundabout. Which exit do you take?

The one on the left?   (Turn to 276)
The one straight ahead?   (Turn to 388)
The one on the right?   (Turn to 288)

68

No money, no jewellery, no weapons of mass destruction. Well what were you expecting to find? There is one thing in the safe, however: a CD-ROM in a plastic case. If it's information you're after, there might be something on it worth looking at. But to access it you'll need to get it back to your computer – turn to 248.

69

He begins to mumble some excuse, but you're not in the mood.

'I'm not sure I can trust you,' you continue. 'Empty your pockets.'

He shamefully pulls out a handkerchief and a clothes brush from his apron, and places them on the table.

'Now go and get on with your work. And if I ever catch you eavesdropping on managerial matters again it will cost you your job,' you bark.

This is enough for the nervous Viv Sprike, who darts past you and out of the door. Ah, the power! I hope you feel good about yourself. Take what you want of your meagre haul and return to 107 to consult your room plan.

70

You slip the weapon into your own breast pocket, making sure the safety catch is on. It's a .45 revolver – make a note of this number on your Fact Sheet for later. If you haven't yet done so, you may go through Victor's jacket pockets by turning to 290. If you think it's time to leave, turn to 281.

71

No chance! Your goalie is completely nutmegged and the ball goes straight through his legs. He's blaming everyone but himself but he's just going to have to put it down to experience. Chalk up a goal to the opposition and carry on with the match. Turn to 319 when ninety minutes are up.

72

You give the map to Eric, who seems pleased to have his crumpled, coffee-stained map back. But as you go to your seat, he calls you back.

'Careful chief – you forgot this,' he tells you, handing you a slip of paper. 'It fell out the map when I opened it.'

It's a small scrap of lined notebook paper with writing on it. But it's not your writing.

You place it carefully in your pocket – copy down what it says on your Fact Sheet. There will be time to have another look at it later, but for now there's a football match to think about. Turn to 356.

73

The bus eventually pulls up in the club car park. Do you get off first and go straight to your office (turn to 302) or wait a while (turn to 83)?

74

Today is the 29th, which means the highly coveted Manager of the Month Award is due to be announced this evening. If Hardwick City FC have been performing well under your guidance, you could be in with a shout.

How many points have you accumulated in your first three matches?

0–6?   (Turn to 192)

7?   (Turn to 37)

9?   (Turn to 15)

75

Are you playing the combination of Will Frost in midfield and Ben Parker up front? If so, turn to 409. Otherwise continue the match as normal, and turn to 76 when it is over.

76

The match is over, leaving only two fixtures remaining this season. Hopefully you're still in with a good chance of winning. To see where you stand, take a look at the rest of the day's results below and complete a new League Table.

```
   Oxton Wanderers 3 — 0 Bridgford City
  Papplewick Town 1 — 2 Epperstone Town
Lowdham Athletic 3 — 1 Gonalston City
    Gunthorpe Utd 1 — 0 Lambley Rovers
```

When you've done that, turn to 432.

77

The free kick is taken, and the ball arcs through the air and into the box where it falls to a Lowdham striker. He takes it on the half-volley and launches a ferocious shot at your goal. Your keeper isn't just beaten — he doesn't even have time to move, and stands there for a few seconds with his mouth open before remembering to shout at the defenders.

That's a goal to them – remember to update your Match Sheet. Seconds after the restart the ref blows to wrap up the match. Turn to 234.

78

Your chosen player has responded exceptionally well in training, and his corners have become longer and more accurate. For the rest of the season, you may add **2** to the dice roll whenever this player takes a corner (make a note of this on your Fact Sheet). Remember: you can focus on two skills this week. If this was your first, turn back to 351 to choose again from the list. If you have now chosen two, turn to 430.

79

Your own kit man, marking your every move! Can you trust anyone in this place?

'Mr Sprike, I cannot tolerate this sort of behaviour at my club,' you proclaim.

The man gapes at you and begins to protest. Do you listen (turn to 145) or refuse to let him speak (turn to 69)?

80

Complete the second half of the fixture in the usual way. When ninety minutes are up, turn to 153.

81

You begin to search swiftly and noiselessly through Sinkowski's desk, systematically examining the contents of each drawer. Statements, stationery, a silver hip-flask — nothing of note. Suddenly you hear the sound of a key being turned in the lock behind you. Turn to 267.

82

You freeze and feel the hairs on your arms stand on end when you see that inside the glove compartment is a small black pistol. Nothing classic about this: just cold, deadly metal. At least

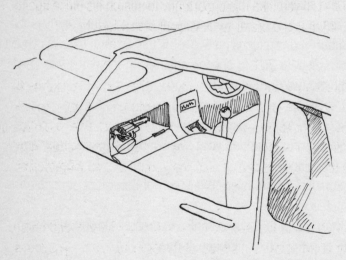

your suspicions are confirmed; after all, what would Sinkowski be doing with such a weapon if he weren't somehow involved in the kidnap of Danny Knox? You almost wish you hadn't found it — but it could be useful. What are you going to do?

Steal the gun? (Turn to 70)
Empty the bullets and replace it? (Turn to 311)
Put it back where you found it? (Turn to 263)

83

You sit and wait while your players file past you and down the steps.

'We're back, guv,' your driver tells you gently. 'Long day, was it?'

'Something like that, Eric,' you reply wearily. He starts telling you about some useless mechanic not being able to fix the carburettor, but you're only half listening as you've spotted club chairman Victor Sinkowski leaving the building and heading towards his car. He hasn't seen you. If you decide to follow him, turn to 441. If you take this opportunity to search his office again, turn to 43. If you'd prefer to leave well alone, turn to 281.

84

Your hands are shaking as you lock the diary safely in your desk drawer. If you've read it carefully you might now be able to narrow down your list of suspects. But there are still eight matches to go, and you're even more determined to win the league now. Return to your room plan at 107 and keep searching if you wish.

85

Wondering where to start, you go to your filing cabinet and reach for your team bus driver's route map for inspiration – you know another club is involved in this mystery somehow, and perhaps it's time you did some detective work.

No map.

But it's always kept here . . . Someone must have been into your office. Do you go in search of it elsewhere in the building (turn to 107)? Or just buy another one before heading up to see your chairman (turn to 371)?

86

This is your opportunity to do some pruning. Is Joe a prize orchid in your team, or just dead wood? Here's how it works. Roll one dice and subtract this number from Joe Fry's Skill. This is the number of millions being offered. If you wish to accept the offer, do so now and remove Joe from your Fact Sheet. Remember to add this new cash to your Budget! If the number is zero or below, it means no one's interested.

You can only attempt this once. When you're ready, turn to 454.

87

Choose a team member to be your free-kick taker. Now roll one dice. If you roll 1–3, turn to 469. If you roll 4–6, turn to 240.

88

Your players come off for half-time, and you walk with them up the tunnel to the dressing room. Is Jonny Steel in your squad? If so, turn to 425. Otherwise turn to 60.

89

You enter the noisy locker room where your squad is preparing for their week's training. You've got an away game against Gonalston City coming up on Saturday afternoon. Do you have a strategy this week?

If you want to concentrate on overall team fitness and discipline, turn to 156.

If you intend to contain the opposition's attack and score on the break, turn to 59.

If you're going to play the possession game, taking rather than creating scoring chances, turn to 159.

If you choose to encourage your team to press forward at every opportunity, turn to 155.

90

Most of the lockers are labelled and shut fast. You read along the familiar names: Duce, Neville, Hoggart, Knox. This is Danny's locker and it's open! A closer look reveals the lock has been forced by someone. What do you do? To open the locker fully, go to 312. To leave well alone, return to consult your room plan on 107.

91

Are you playing Frost or Leslie in your team for this match? If so, turn to 63. Otherwise turn to 103.

92

Your chosen keeper has responded well in training. For the rest of the season, whenever the opposing team scores a goal, roll two dice. If you roll 2, 3 or 4, treat the shot as saved. Make a note of this on your Fact Sheet next to this player's name (it only applies if he is in goal). Remember: you can focus on two skills this week. If this was your first, turn back to 351 to choose again from the list. If you have now chosen two, turn to 430.

93

You swing left on to Chestnut Drive, narrower than the last road. Here, the warehouses give way to lock-ups and small industrial units. But you're worried you're driving yourself into a dead end, and about the single headlight that has just flickered into view behind you. Before long you're faced with yet another cross-roads. Where to now?

Left on to Birch Close?   (Turn to 133)
Ahead on to Neville Close?   (Turn to 292)
Right on to Bonner Hill?   (Turn to 332)

94

There are nearly two hundred square feet of goal to aim for, and your striker misses all of them. Instead the ball whizzes high over the crossbar and knocks a meat pie out of the hands of an elderly Hardwick supporter. No points for that. Turn to 213.

95

You enter the bar and are hit by a wall of heat and noise. The large room is filled with small, round tables surrounded by high stools, most of which are occupied by Gunthorpe's young crowd. A bar runs the length of the far wall, and above it is a row of TV screens showing different sporting events. The one attracting the most interest is the replay of Gunthorpe's win this afternoon. You head over to the quieter end of the bar, where there is an older gent sitting alone and a barman in a black apron polishing glasses.

'Can I help you?' he asks cordially.

'I hope so. It's information I'm after,' you tell him, trying not to sound suspicious but failing. 'A meeting took place on Wednesday 9th between two men – one of them fat, bald, cigar-smoking – probably in a suit. I was wondering if you saw them.'

The barman narrows his eyes at you.

'Maybe. You going to do the decent thing and make this worth my while?' he says sardonically, winking at the old man sitting next to you.

Well, are you? If you pay him for information – a hundred should do it – turn to 225. If you prefer not to, turn to 10.

96

Before you can look any further you are startled by an icy voice behind you.

'Can I help you?'

The speaker is a short, thin lady in her seventies, dressed in a blue woollen suit and a string of expensive-looking pearls. She's holding a clutch of leads, at the end of which are three scrawny Shi-Tzu dogs in ridiculous tartan coats.

'I was looking for Victor. I'm his – nephew,' you lie.

'Well, I haven't seen you before,' the woman answers brusquely. 'And anyway, Mr Sinkowski is away.'

One of the rat-dogs starts growling pathetically.

'Oh, well, I'd better come back another time then. Goodbye!'

You force a grin, but her face remains stony. Better get going before you become the next subject of a Neighbourhood Watch meeting. Head back to your office and turn to 392.

97

'He'll calm down eventually,' you tell yourself. But the trouble is, he expected you to have a go at him – and when you didn't he thought that meant his behaviour was justified. Bad move: sometimes you have to take the role of disciplinarian with these players. Whenever you play Steve Fitzgerald in future, roll one dice before the match. If you roll a 1, 2 or 3 it means he picks up a yellow card in the first fifteen minutes for his poor conduct towards the officials. Make a note of this on your Fact Sheet so you don't forget. Now turn to 129.

98

The two players concerned are Anthony Bostock and Jed Stevens. Both players are now injured, and you must roll in the normal way to see if they can recover in time for the next match (see Player Recovery on page 9). Bad luck. Hopefully you've kept back enough players to fill their boots. Turn to 412.

99

You are about to close the locker when you have an idea. You take a handful of small change from your pocket and select a ten-pence coin. By jamming it under the sheet metal you eventually manage to lever it upwards. Underneath is a small, leather-bound diary. You take the book, close the locker door and quickly leave the room. If you wish you may turn to 115 to read the diary before going back to 107 and the room plan.

100

Bill Drebble has duly been announced as this month's best manager, with his impressive goal average and disciplinary record. You missed it by a gnat's whisker. Fax him your congratulations if you wish, and try not to feel too envious. But you feel buoyed having come so close, so add **1** Morale. Then turn to 347.

101

You have failed this time! But there's always a second chance. Perhaps you've learned some important things along the way. So when you're ready, gather your wits and go back to the beginning for another chance to be the Big Match Manager.

102

The weapon you took is locked in your desk drawer. If you move he'll shoot you.

'You were stupid to take my gun,' he tells you. 'It's very easy to get hold of another one, if you know the right people.'

Turn to 4.

103

On the way to the Gonalston City stadium you study the form of the opposition.

***

Gonalston City FC
Overall Skill: 67

Gonalston have enjoyed a windfall of new talent this season, and with two big wins under their belts already they're looking like a force to be reckoned with. Jules Torrence will be looking to crush Hardwick at home in this match, and you'll have to play at full tilt if you're going to deny him.

***

You know what to do by now. Calculate your Match Factor for this away game, then see if you can snatch an important away victory here today. If at any point during the match you are awarded a free kick, turn to 18. If not, when the referee blows for full-time you may turn to 377.

104

She makes a note in her book, and continues with an innocent smile, 'There are a lot of conspiracy theories around at the moment.' Then her smile disappears. 'Do you think someone you know might be behind this?'

You reply quickly. 'No comment.' You stare at her, and she stares right back, eyebrows raised.

Questions from other reporters follow thick and fast. You answer them as best you can, ending the meeting half an hour later. Do you try to speak to Anna Julian in private? If so, turn to 106. If you wish to head back to your office, turn to 471.

105

After three or four miles of furious driving there's still no sign of him. Either he's way ahead of you by now or you made a wrong turn. Best cut your losses and head back to the club – turn to 281.

106

'Ms Julian,' you say gently as she is preparing to leave. 'Could you tell me what you meant by your question?'

She looks startled for a moment before speaking.

'Just what I said. You must agree this is a weird business. A rich player, a manager desperate for his safe return, yet two weeks later and no ransom demand? I –' She glances around. 'Look, I'm sorry, I have to go.'

She grabs her notes and rushes off. You know Anna is right, but you still feel there is something she isn't telling you.

Turn to 471.

107

So where are you going to start? Below is the plan of the Hardwick City FC main building. You may visit any of the rooms by turning to the number marked on the map, but remember the number of this paragraph as you will have to return here after each room you visit. After you have tried **six** locations, turn immediately to 205.

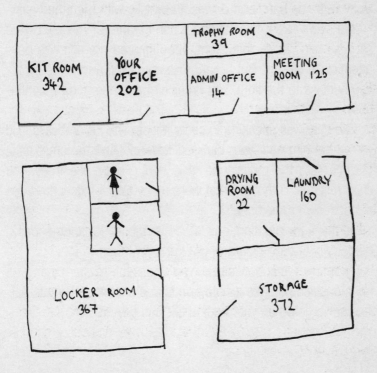

108

You turn the wheel to 20, then 24, then 64. There is a barely audible click from inside as the tumblers fall into place. You take the key you found in Victor's office and insert it in the lock. It turns, and the heavy door swings open. Turn to 68.

109

'I might have better ears than him,' he tells you in a gruff voice. He is wearing a tweed jacket buttoned up to the collar and has a grubby beard that might have been ginger once.

You reach into your wallet for another bribe, but he waves it away with one hand and downs his whisky with the other.

'You seem like a decent sort, I don't want yer money. I were sat next yer friends that night. They ignored me. No one pays attention to old Bill. But I 'eard.' He chuckles, and holds up his empty glass to the light. You order him another, and he continues.

'Like they was speaking in code, it was. The fat one says, "So you've got him near your club, but where?" And the other fella, the one with the moustache, tells him, "Follow the trees, you can't miss us." I thought that were funny talk – follow the trees – that's 'ow I remember.'

You thank the old man, and leave him money for another drink. He nods in appreciation and you leave for home.

The fat one must be Victor . . . so who is the mystery man with the moustache? Make a note of this and anything else interesting you've heard on your Fact Sheet and turn to 358.

110

You slowly insert the key into the lock and turn it sharply to the left. Nothing. It won't budge, and now you've bent it. Are you going to leave it there (turn to 186) or try to get it out (turn to 435)?

111

It's the 76th minute and the game is running smoothly after a period of calm. But Gunthorpe have been fighting hard for territory, and Hoggart loses a midfield tussle with the Gunthorpe centre-back – who slots through a clever little pass to their attacking midfielder. The home crowd are on their feet and for a moment Gunthorpe look to be in with a chance as their players press forward in numbers. But the roar suddenly dies away as the ball is expertly collected in the box by Antek Bobak, who darts forward and whips a cross out wide to John Hoggart on the right wing. Gunthorpe left gaping holes in their defence when they powered forward for their last attack, and Toby Wood is quick to capitalise as he makes a single-minded run down the centre of the pitch. A sole defender is useless when a counter-measure like this is employed correctly, and Hoggart and Wood are stride for stride now. Roll one dice. If you roll 1–4, turn to 31. If you roll 5 or 6, turn to 467.

112

The colour drains from your cheeks as Victor walks into your office, shutting the door behind him with one hand, pointing a small black pistol at your stomach with the other. Your chairman smiles wanly at you.

'You had to get involved, didn't you?' he sighs. 'His time was up,' he says, indicating Danny with the barrel of the gun, 'but you could have stayed alive just by keeping your head down and getting on with your job.'

He takes a yellow handkerchief from his trouser pocket and pats sweat from his forehead before continuing.

'You and the players think all this football is so very special, but don't you see? It's just a business like any other. And the point of business is to get rich. Nothing is going to stop me from making my millions. Jack and I have been planning this for over a year now.' Here he levels his gun at Danny's head. 'And this is one game we don't intend to lose.'

Have you come across a gun belonging to Victor before? If so, add the gun's number to this paragraph number and turn to that number. If not, turn to 4.

113

The Bridgford player is in plenty of space and makes a beeline for goal. Two Hardwick defenders are racing towards him for all they're worth, but it's too late and your keeper knows it. He rushes off his line to close the angle and meet the attacker head-on. Roll two dice. If you roll 9 or more, turn to 270. If you roll less than 9, turn to 346.

114

You follow him cautiously through the exit and on to the one-way system. You are queuing at lights, and you can just make out his sausage fingers drumming on the steering-wheel two cars ahead. Your heart is thumping in your chest as you pray your car can keep pace with the powerful engine under Sinkowski's bonnet. After an age the lights turn to green. Do you:

Keep up to make sure you don't lose him?   (Turn to 27)

Hang back to make sure he doesn't see you?   (Turn to 468)

Decide against playing these games and return to your office?

(Turn to 281)

115

Safely back in your office, you lock the door behind you and open the small book. You feel uncomfortable reading poor Danny's private diary, but it might contain important clues. Turning to his last entry, you begin to read.

Monday 3rd.
Meeting with VS and JT at the Holly. V said it was to discuss my future at Hardwick but I shouldn't tell boss – that was weird. When I got there I knew something was wrong, V very nervous. Couldn't believe it when J said they wanted me to *stop* scoring so his team could win. Creepy little swine offered me a million. No way I'm throwing matches for anyone but pretended I was interested. Could hardly eat a thing. Don't know what to do. Want to tell boss but what if they find out? V said things could get hard for me if I make wrong decision. Went home early but didn't tell Jo. Oh God I'm scared.

Make a note of this paragraph on your Fact Sheet for future reference and turn to 84.

116

By the end of the training week you have seen a genuine improvement in your midfield. The players are anticipating well and passing the ball around confidently. For the next match only, add **1** to the Skill of any two of your Midfielders. Turn to 34.

117

You feel like whooping as you see the dark silhouette of your assailant receding in the murky night. But it doesn't take long before you realise why only one man was shooting at you. The other had run back to his car, which – thanks to a souped-up engine and reinforced bonnet – is gaining on you right now. A single dim headlight, half hanging off, is clearly getting bigger in your mirror as you reach a crossroads. Time for a moment of clarity. You've brought no weapon with you, and you're being pursued by an assassin. Where exactly are you going to go? It's a crossroads; that means you've got three options.

Left on to Bridge Lane? (Turn to 455)

Ahead on to Shuttleworth Road? (Turn to 227)

Right on to Elm Avenue? (Turn to 460)

118

You spend a couple of hours sifting through the paperwork. Eric Redman at Lambley Rovers has expressed an interest in buying

Toby Wood, and José Torrego at Woodborough is keen to buy Ricky Neville. Among the players for sale, the following two stand out:

Ivan Najev

Position: Midfielder (Skill 7)   Last Season's Stats:
Born: Dubrovnik 11/3/86   Goals: 1
Height: 6ft 2in   Yellow Cards: 2
Weight: 12st 2lb   Red Cards: 0

Croatia has a wealth of footballing talent, and Najev is one of the stars. He used to be a waiter in a seaside restaurant until he was spotted by a talent scout; Ivan hung up his apron and never looked back. He plays typical east European football: fast, showy and intimidating.

Richard Corner

Position: Defender (Skill 6)   Last Season's Stats:
Born: London 16/5/80   Goals: 0
Height: 6ft 6in   Yellow Cards: 3
Weight: 13st 9lb   Red Cards: 1

Richard Corner's long stride and height make him an ideal defender against most attacks. He has an artistic temperament which needs the firm backing of his team and his manager, but when he's settled with a club he turns in a star performance.

For the second time this season, the transfer market is open. But remember you can only buy new players if you have enough money left in your Budget. What do you want to do first?

Consider selling Toby Wood?   (Turn to 282)
Consider selling Ricky Neville?   . (Turn to 238)

Put in a bid for Ivan Najev?   (Turn to 464)
Put in a bid for Richard Corner?   (Turn to 251)
If you're keeping things the way they are, turn to 244.

119

Good speech. That's fired them up. Add **1** Morale, then turn to 34.

120

'What do you think you're doing?' you boom.

He almost jumps out of his skin when he hears your voice, and immediately starts protesting his innocence; but you've caught him red-handed and you can't have an employee subverting Hardwick City like this. You give him twenty minutes to clear out his belongings, and have security escort him off the premises. That's one little problem solved. Back in your office you pour yourself a black coffee and rest for a while – it's been a long day. But isn't it about time you went to see your chairman as he requested? He's waiting for you at 236.

121

Question: what happens when an unstoppable force hits an immoveable object? Answer: it's a draw. A point apiece, which you should be content with in an away match. See how the rest of the league is going on paragraph 411.

122

You may add **2** to your dice roll. Salvatore Duce is an expert penalty-taker. Turn to 348.

123

In the dying seconds of the game, a Lowdham midfielder picks out their man on the wing with a looping cross. Steve Fitzgerald is alert and has it covered, but there is a duel in the air for possession and a clash of heads. The linesman is well-placed, his flag goes up and a free kick is awarded to Lowdham. Steve is incensed at the decision and storms over to the ref to protest. Stupid boy – he's earned himself a yellow card for complaining! Everyone knows you don't talk back to the man in black; but here's one of your own men, earning a fortune on the field and still having tantrums. Is Fitzy on a yellow card already? If so, turn to 452. If not turn to 169.

124

Your strength up front is leaving Bridgford's defenders in disarray. Your attackers are breaking forward at every opportunity and their goalie is having a nightmare as shots come in from all sides. You may add **3** to your Match Factor for the remainder of this match. Now turn to 214.

125

In the centre of this large room is a polished walnut table surrounded by twelve high-backed chairs. Around the walls are portraits of Hardwick's great players from years gone by. Otherwise the room is empty. Return to the room plan at 107.

126

You take the second exit and find yourself on open road. Turn to 105.

127

Your chosen keeper has responded well in training. For the rest of the season, whenever the opposing team scores a goal, roll two dice. If you roll 2 or 3, treat the shot as saved. Make a note of this on your Fact Sheet next to this player's name (it only applies if he is in goal). Remember: you can focus on two skills this week. If this was your first, turn back to 351 to choose again from the list. If you have now chosen two, turn to 430.

128

You stand at the edge of your dugout flapping your arms around and shouting at the players to press forward, pass the ball and use their common sense. But you're putting off the linesman, and a couple of minutes into the match you're outraged when he completely ignores a clear foul on your wing-back. Are you going to tell him what you think of his decision (turn to 206) or bite your tongue and let him get on with it (turn to 193)?

129

Your first match is over. Did your team
Win?   (Turn to 416)
Draw?   (Turn to 293)
Lose?   (Turn to 355)

130

'Some people believe in God, others believe in the tooth fairy,' you continue, inspired.

'I'm agnostic,' says Ricky Neville.

'Oh, make the tea,' mocks John Hoggart.

'I believe in teamwork!' you exclaim, extending your arms to your players who are hanging on your every word now. You pause, eyes shining, and raise your voice.

'Call me a romantic. But when you go out there on Saturday I want to see eleven men working as one man. Eleven minds dreaming of one victory. Ask not what your team can do for you. Ask what you can do for your team!'

'Yes, Master Chief!' Steve Fitzgerald leaps to his feet and salutes.

'Il ressemble beaucoup à Charles de Gaulle,' Dmitri Duval mutters, shaking his head in wonder.

Roll one dice. If you roll 1–3, turn to 119. If you roll 4–6, turn to 24.

131

Saturday 15th

It's the day of the big match against Lowdham Athletic. You drive straight to your home ground to make final decisions on your team and prepare a pre-match talk. Better not tell them about last night – they're shaken up enough by Danny's disappearance.

It's time to select your 11 players for the match. Remember you must pick at least two Defenders, two Midfielders and two Attackers. Write down the ones you pick on your first Match

Sheet, which you'll find on page 206. When you're ready, turn to 179.

132

They say a week's a long time in football, and that's nearly how long you've got. What do you want to concentrate on this week? If you have a particular player you would like to single out for special attention, turn to 463. If you think overall team fitness is a more important issue, turn to 265.

133

You turn the car on to Birch Close, and instantly regret it. Dead ahead is a high gate made of steel mesh and topped with razor wire. To either side of you are a dozen or so densely-packed, flat-roofed buildings with no gaps between them. Behind you is the only moving thing in this desolate landscape: the silent, solitary spot of a headlight emerging from the gloom at the top of the road. You're cornered, and the driver knows it as he creeps the car forward to within twelve feet of you. Are you in possession of a bleeper? If so, turn to 273. Otherwise turn to 162.

134

Whatever gave you that idea? And where are you going to look – *Yellow Pages*? It sounds like you're clutching at straws now. Drive back home the way you came and turn to 358.

135

For the next match only, add **1** to the Skill of any two of your Attackers. Turn to 6.

136

Unfortunately the players aren't showing any signs of backing down, and several punches are thrown before the match officials can intervene. Roll two dice and take the difference between them. This is the number of players that have been injured from your team and must now be substituted. Now do the same for your opponents. Remember neither side may make more than three substitutions!

Spend the interval focusing your team and calming their nerves, then resume the match. When you hear the full-time whistle, turn to 61.

137

'Calm down, calm down,' you say, wading into the fray. You narrowly miss a swinging fist as you try to put yourself between your players and theirs. 'This is a professional football stadium, not a school yard!' you exclaim. 'Do you think the England team would ever behave like this?' The players hang their heads in shame. 'I don't care who started it, get to the dressing room, the lot of you.'

By now the match officials have turned up to defuse the situation. But you narrowly averted some quite unnecessary trouble with your discipline and fairness. Good work – guess that's why you're the boss!

Spend the interval focusing your team and calming their nerves, then resume the match. When you hear the full-time whistle, turn to 61.

138

Well, Sherlock. It looks like you're on your way to uncovering a major crime ring. It's clearer than ever that Victor's at the centre of all this, along with his accomplice *JT*. Danny's disappearance, the strange events at the other football clubs – it would seem that these two cheats would stop at nothing to see a certain team go top of the league so they can rake in the millions. It makes your blood boil to think that Victor would happily watch his own club fail just so he can top up his salary. And as for poor José Torrego and Jules Torrence, whose teams have been attacked for the same reason – well, you know how they feel.

You feel suddenly alone as you realise you still can't go to the police. You've no hard evidence, Danny is still in danger, and you doubt these people would hesitate in killing him. But you're getting close, and as long as Victor thinks you suspect nothing you can stay ahead of the game. Hopefully he won't notice his safe is empty . . .

You spend the weekend at home. Turn to 289.

139

You've got a home game coming up against Bridgford City this Saturday. This could be a good time to work on some individual skills. Alternatively you may wish to concentrate on overall Morale and Fitness in the team. The choice is yours.

Individual skills   (Turn to 351)
Morale and Fitness   (Turn to 335)

140

'This is a home game, and I don't need to remind you that the majority of accidents occur in the home,' you remind them. 'Sloppiness has been the undoing of many an army, but that's not going to happen here today. Liquid passing and a solid defence *can* co-exist. Such is the physics of football.'

'Genius, Einstein!' applauds Steve Fitzgerald.

'What ees fizzics?' asks Salvatore; but your back line has got the message. Add **1** to the Skill of any two of your Defenders for this match only, and play out the game in the usual way. When you reach the 30th minute, turn to 75.

141

Before you can even reach through the hole a hollow, piercing clamour echoes all around you. The cops are going to be round here like a shot! Quick – beat a hasty retreat through the bushes and get back on the main road before anyone sees you. You've got a long walk back to your office. When you get there, turn to 392.

142

The two players concerned are Antek Bobak and John Hoggart. Both players are now injured, and you must roll in the normal way to see if they can recover in time for the next match (see page 9). Bad luck. Hopefully you've kept back enough players to fill their boots. Turn to 412.

143

'I don't make promises like that,' you tell him sternly. 'If I haven't played you it's because you haven't proved yourself on the field. In my team it's goal or dole.'

Ian's response is unequivocal. 'In that case I want to be put on the transfer list.'

Right or wrong, Ian sees himself as a star of the future and you've upset him. You must now subtract **2** from Ian's Skill in any match he plays for you until you get the opportunity to sell him to another club. Turn to 352.

144

For the next match only, add **2** to the Skill of any two of your Attackers but subtract **1** from each of your Defenders. Turn to 6.

145

You tell Viv Sprike that you want an explanation before you decide what to do with him. He stands looking at his feet for a while before speaking.

'I'm sorry, boss, I just wanted to make sure you're not on – well, on the wrong side.'

'Of course not!' you protest. 'But how do I know I can trust you?'

'Keep your voice down,' he hisses. 'These walls are paper-thin and your office is certainly bugged by now.' He shifts uncomfortably as you let him continue. 'Danny's in danger, more than you know. These people – look, I can't say for sure, but I've heard stuff. A conversation upstairs. "Unit 29, that's where we've got him."'

Viv pauses before continuing.

'You better be careful, they'll be on to me soon. Thanks for listening, boss. Take this, I'll come help if I can.' And he hands you a black bleeper before darting past you and out the door.

You are left alone in the kit room. Make a note of the bleeper and anything else important on your Fact Sheet. When you've done that you may turn back to the room plan at 107 to keep searching.

146

'Right, you lot. Now I've seen some lousy defending before, but nothing like this. And as for you strikers, I'm paying you to score goals, not flap about like a pair of wet fish. Erm – not to worry – you've a mountain to climb, and it's going to be an uphill struggle, so go out there and salvage what you can from this dog's dinner.'

Oh dear. You're not very good at this. Subtract **1** from your team's Morale. Remember this will bring down your Match Factor by 1 as well! When you're ready, turn to 448.

147

You decide to give yourself a break. You've been working hard, and haven't had time for what you really like to do now and again – to get stuck into a big plate of ham sandwiches and the sports stories in the press. But your players are none too happy.

'What's going on, boss – are you ill?' Ben Parker asks you later in the week.

'Obviously got no time for us these days,' you overhear Ant Bostock grumbling to Steve Fitzgerald, who replies bitterly, 'Is this some kind of punishment?'

What were you thinking? A successful manager must be seen to be working as hard as the players themselves. Your hands-off attitude has alienated the team: lose **2** Morale and **1** Fitness. Now turn to 34.

148

A long ball up the field picks out their man on the left wing, who controls it with ease. Your men look tired and fail to close him down, and he makes a run towards your eighteen-yard line unchallenged. Your solid No. 4 shirt is waiting for him there, but a neat little one-two leaves your hapless defender for dead and their striker finds himself in acres of space. Your goalie has committed himself and charges off his line to throw himself on the ball, but catches the striker's ankle instead. You see it all in slow motion and know what's coming. 'Pheeeep!' goes the referee's shrill whistle, and he points with conviction to the spot. Your players protest, but it's no use; Papplewick's aggressive manoeuvre has earned them a penalty in the dying moments of the game. Roll one dice. If you roll 1–3, turn to 226. If you roll 4–6 turn to 58.

149

You open the door to the phonebox. Everything seems normal, but suddenly you spot something small and squarish near your foot. Do you want to pick it up (turn to 450), or would you prefer to get back in your car and follow the trail of oil (turn to 28)?

150

The shot is low and hard. The keeper dives the right way but he can't get close to the ball as it punches into the back of the netting. A goal to you, fair and square: chalk it up while the players revel in the glory. Then turn to 213.

151

'Any one of you could leave now and it wouldn't make a blind bit of difference.'

'You're a bag of laughs,' mutters Antek Bobak, but you continue.

'We're all cogs in the machine of this great football club which is bigger than all of us. Saturday's game is just like any other. Heads down, work hard and do your job. No arguments.'

The players look at each other with disquiet. Well, that went down like a cup of cold sick. What are you on? Lose **1** Morale as you've made your players feel unappreciated. Now turn to 34.

152

'Er – Eric,' you say to your coach driver as innocently as you can. 'Would you mind dropping me off here? I need to go and see – ah – someone about, erm, something.'

But Eric doesn't even seem to care.

'Right you are, guv'nor,' he chirps, and the door opens with a hiss. 'See you on Monday.'

The jam isn't moving and you step out on to the pavement. You walk away hurriedly, but looking back at the bus even your players don't seem to have noticed your odd behaviour. They must be tired after the game. Turn to 466.

153

Here are the results from the rest of the day's matches.

```
    Lowdham Athletic 0 — 1 Epperstone Town
      Lambley Rovers 2 — 0 Gonalston City
       Gunthorpe Utd 3 — 0 Papplewick Town
 Woodborough County 2 — 1 Oxton Wanderers
```

When you've finished completing the weekend's League Table, turn to 272.

154

What is it you're looking for?

A sports bar	(Turn to 42)
A hotel	(Turn to 314)
A private detective	(Turn to 134)

155

'If I've seen this team once I've seen them a hundred times,' you begin telling your squad in a commanding voice, 'and their defence is atrocious. We're going out there to win points on Saturday, and what do points mean?'

'A superior league position,' chant your eager squad.

'Correct. I want you to impress the crowd. Every pass you make, and every kick you take; every time you break, and every dive you fake they'll be watching you. Be ambitious. Be dynamic. Be yourselves.' Your players nod vigorously in appreciation. But how will they respond in training? Roll one dice.

If you roll 1 or 2, turn to 144.

If you roll 3 or 4, turn to 135.
If you roll 5 or 6, turn to 334.

156

'We're going to spend the week doing some circuit training, dribbling practice and clean tackling,' you tell your players when they've filed into the dressing room. They let out a groan.

'Can't we practise penalties?' asks Ben Parker, lining up an imaginary spot-kick and taking a punt.

'Why must we run around like chickens?' whines Dmitri Duval. 'I just want to play ze beautiful game.'

But you ignore the protests, as you know what's best for them. Work your players hard and add **2** to Fitness. And for the next match only, you may ignore any cards shown to your players as you have taught them to play in a more disciplined way. Now turn to 6.

157

Are there bullets in that gun he's holding? If you have already emptied them out, turn to 461. If you stole a gun from his car, turn to 102.

158

Take a look at your new League Table. With only one game remaining, there is only one question: can you still win or not? If you're at the top of the table, or within 3 points of it, turn to 171. If you're too far behind, turn to 189.

159

'It's an away game and they'll be trying to undo us in the middle,' you advise. 'And as all good footballers know, what's the best form of defence?'

'Midfield,' chorus your players, except the defenders who look confused.

'Correct. I want tight passing, quick interception, and no heroics; but above all, common sense.' You tap the side of your head with your finger and the squad murmur their understanding. But how will they respond in training? Roll one dice.

If you roll 1, 2 or 3, turn to 47.

If you roll 4, 5 or 6, turn to 338.

160

The laundry room. There is a large pile of sweaty kit on the floor, waiting to be washed. Do you wish to search through it? If so turn to 349. If you'd rather hold your nose and leave, return to 107 and the room plan.

161

Your players are all ears and you address them in a loud voice.

'Gunthorpe will be hurting from their last match,' you begin, 'but they're always a team to carry a goal threat.'

'We can have 'em!' shouts Will Frost excitedly, and the players murmur their agreement.

'For every goal they get, I get *due* goal!' adds Salvatore Duce, punching the air.

'I like you, Dukey,' you say kindly. 'But I like a clean sheet more. This is an away game, and that means they'll not be giving anything away. United will be asking questions and I want to make sure you're ready with the answers.'

Roll one dice. If you roll 1, turn to 183. If you roll 2–6, turn to 23.

162

Shame. You got all this way. Danny is only a few metres from where you're sitting right now, but you're cornered and defenceless. The man who is getting out of the car behind you is fitting a silencer to the end of his handgun, but it wouldn't matter if he didn't. There's no one around here to help you. He takes aim at the back of your neck. Your body will be bagged up with stones and dumped in the river tonight. Turn to 101.

163

The goalkeeper reacts with lightning speed, flinging his body sideways just in time to get his fingertips to the ball. Unlucky, but a great move – and you've forced a corner. Roll for this corner as you normally would (where 6 = goal), then play out the rest of the game. When it's over you can turn to 377.

164

'Twist the bottle and not the cork,' you remember from somewhere, and you pour yourself a glass. Quietly now – you wouldn't want a loud pop telling all your kind secretaries next door that you're hitting the bottle at 9:30 on a Monday morning. But it's delicious and refreshing, and you feel good! Every manager deserves a bit of a treat once in a while. You kick off your shoes and rock back in your chair to make yourself comfortable, and then immediately rock forward again as you pass out face on desk. Turn to 305.

165
You sit in the driver's seat of your car. You feel uneasy . . . But you drive out of town anyway and in a few minutes you find yourself waiting at traffic lights on the ring road. The black saloon which has been following you since you left the car park pulls alongside you, and a man in a brown suit winds down his window to ask directions. As you wind down yours, the friendly smile withers from his face and your last sight on this earth is the silenced muzzle of his revolver. The first patrol car to pass is half an hour later. The ambulance arrives pitifully late. Turn to 101.

166
You turn the key, still in the ignition, praying the engine isn't flooded. The plugs fire but you're too hasty on the clutch, and the car lurches forward into the middle of the crossroads and dies. You glance into your wing mirror; the men have broken into a trot now they've realised you're trying to make a run for it. On the next attempt you're luckier, and two things happen together. First, the engine roars into life and the tyres spin on wet tarmac as you slip the clutch. Second, your back windscreen shatters as one of the men empties half his revolver in your direction. You take off down the street, pulse racing, as three more bullets rip into the metal of your car, missing the fuel tank by vital inches.

Turn to 117.

167

Something about that message . . . You rewind the tape, turn the volume to maximum, and press play.

'Danny! It's me – don't move, I'm on my way.' Your own voice on tape booms over the hissing on the cassette. Then the screech of tyres, and again a thud. But this time you can make out two new voices, very faint:

'He's out col . . . '

'Good . . . ork. Now let's . . . et him back to the ware . . . se bef . . . he . . . ies to . . . cape again.'

'Hey – put th . . . pho . . . ack. It looks . . . picious.' Then the click as the receiver is replaced.

Now turn to 451.

168

You arrive back at Hardwick and the security guard at the gate does a double take when he sees the familiar face of Danny Knox sweep by. You take him to your office, and sit him down with a coffee and blankets from the medical room.

'This should make the duty sergeant's night,' you say as you begin dialling the police station. 'You'll need a proper check-up too.'

But there's no dialling tone. Looking down, you can see why. The phone cord has been neatly snipped off at the wall. And as you stand holding the useless receiver, the door to your office swings open.

Turn to 112.

169

Add up the Skill of your Defenders. Is the total

Below 15?   (Turn to 77)

15 or more?   (Turn to 320)

170

Ricky is pleased to be singled out for praise. The same cannot be said for the remainder of the defence, who are demoralised by your words.

'What is wrong with us, boss?' complains Antek Bobak. 'We work hard too!'

Bad move. For the next match only, add **1** to Ricky's Skill but subtract **1** from the Skill of whichever Defenders play alongside him. Better keep player talks where they belong – in private. Now turn to 34.

171

Maybe it's all going to be decided by the last game of the season. Maybe your position in the league is already unassailable! But I hope you haven't forgotten all about your best striker – the one who's not been seen for nine long weeks? Time to head for home and consider your options. Turn to 262.

172

You turn the paper to the back page as you always do, and you are shocked to see some familiar faces looking very much the worse for wear. One has a split lip and a torn ear, another appears to have had his nose broken and all three have black eyes. 'Gonalston Thugs In Nightclub Brawl' reads the headline.

'Just before midnight on Saturday,' the story continues, 'three members of title hopefuls Gonalston City were seen fighting outside The Black Orchid nightspot. One eyewitness has described all three men as "ripped to the britches on booze". They are currently recovering in hospital.'

You're playing Gonalston on Saturday! They should be easy to beat now, and it serves them right, you can't help thinking with a smile. But then your ringing phone startles you and you pick it up. It's none other than Jules Torrence, Gonalston's manager.

Turn to 387.

173

'Welcome to another feast of football. We're live at Gunthorpe, where title hopefuls Hardwick City are about to get us under way In what promises to be a thrilling fixture.'

When play reaches the 75th minute, turn to 291.

174

'Sorry Eric, I haven't seen it,' you tell the driver. He closes the door and begins to pull away, grumbling about having to buy a new one. Turn to 356.

175

You may now look at the letter from the FA (turn to 394), open the brown paper parcel (turn to 316), leaf through the *Hardwick Herald* (turn to 172), or forget the post and go to talk to your players (turn to 89).

176

Turn to 154.

177

Eventually the amber light begins to flash and the car in front pulls away. You floor the accelerator and overtake, wishing you'd had that eye test as you scan the distance for any sign of Victor Sinkowski. There's a roundabout up ahead, but still no sign of him as you reach it. Do you take:

The exit on the left?	(Turn to 276)
The exit straight ahead?	(Turn to 388)
The exit on the right?	(Turn to 288)

178

'It's me,' says the low voice of your chairman.

There is a short pause before he continues.

'Of course. Everything's going as planned.' You can't make out what the tinny voice on the other end of the line is saying, but whoever it is sounds agitated.

'I told you when we met in Gunthorpe, and I'm telling you again now,' Victor goes on confidently. 'Doesn't suspect a thing. Look, a competent manager maybe, but otherwise an idiot.'

He's talking about you! Your cheeks burn as he continues.

'Yes, we're sticking to the plans I showed you, and yes, they're at my house and quite safe. In the safe.' He gives a gurgling chuckle at his own joke, and you hear the rattle of ice as he takes a long pull on his drink. 'It's double-locked, once with a key which I have here, twice with a combination. Only one other person knew that, and you know what happened to her. Now stop worrying, I'll take care of business this end. You just see to the week's events. Torrego still thinks he's a big fish and it's time to reel him in. I'll see you at the weekend.'

The two men exchange pleasantries and Victor hangs up. You listen intently as he finishes his drink, picks up his jacket and leaves the room.

Make a note of any details you think might be important, then turn to 203.

179

Lowdham Athletic FC
Overall Skill: 66
Lowdham sometimes let themselves down by sloppy passing, but this is balanced out by sheer pace and goal-scoring ability. Unbeaten in five matches, their morale is high, and club manager Bill Drebble reckons they're in with a real chance this season.

It's 2:30pm in the dressing room and the roar of your home fans is deafening. The noise seems to have lifted the spirits of your team, and it remains only for you to send them out with a common purpose.

'All I am concerned about is making a good showing of ourselves and trying to get a result,' you start telling your eager players. 'This one is going to be hard. It will be an uphill grind, but we have to make sure we're solid and brave, while we're also going to need spirit, heart and guts.'

Do you tell them to:

'Play a passing game, try to contain the opposition and keep possession'? (Turn to 381)

'Keep the defence tight, try to keep a clean sheet and not leave ourselves open at the back'? (Turn to 465)

'Focus on the back of their net, apply pressure on their back four, but most of all go out there and have a good time'? (Turn to 310)

180

You make your way up the stairs to the executive floor and steal quietly up to the door of the club's chairman and your boss, Mr Victor Sinkowski. You check up and down the carpeted landing but it's deserted. You press your ear to the door and it's quite silent apart from the thumping of your heart in your chest. The key slips smoothly into the lock, and the door swings open. Turn to 9.

181

Pheeeeeep! The shrill whistle sounds and the ball is kicked for the first time. The Wanderers stadium is packed with the distinctive blue and black of their supporters, but your fans are out in force too and singing away merrily behind the Oxton goal. What type of manager are you?

One who strides up and down the touchline shouting orders? (Turn to 128)

One who sits quietly, letting the players get on with the job? (Turn to 424)

182

You open the door and climb out, intending to give yourself up. Maybe this has all been a case of mistaken identity? But your doubts disappear for ever when your murderer levels his gun at your head and fires. By the time he is telling his accomplice how easy you were, your body is already lifeless.

Turn to 101.

183

During the course of the week, your defence tightens and groups together well. But your attackers seem unwilling to make forward moves, and appear to be hanging back more than usual. For the next match only, add **2** to the Skill of one of your Defenders but subtract **1** from the Skill of two of your playing Attackers.

Turn to 34.

184

In that case, you must be in possession of a brass key with a number on it. Turn to that number now. Otherwise stop cheating and turn to 392.

185

You're standing in a clean, empty garage with whitewashed walls. There are shelves along one side carrying an array of gardening tools, and a cupboard is set into the far wall. The only door is the one you came in by.

Do you open the cupboard (turn to 7) or get out while you can and return to your office (turn to 392)?

186

Viv's a resourceful man and he's going to have to try to get it out himself. You've got better things to do – like manage your team to the top of the league for starters! Go back to your office and hope Mr Sprike doesn't mind. Turn to 398.

187

You reach under the garage door and pull. It's not locked! The mechanism is well oiled and the door slides smoothly along its runners. You look around for observers but you're safely shielded by the apple trees. In a moment you're inside with the door shut safely behind you. Turn to 185.

188

You've got Victor's car well within your sights now and he does-n't seem to have noticed you. You tail him over more lights and a couple of roundabouts, then on to a dual carriageway. Wherever he's going he doesn't seem to be in much of hurry. After five minutes he indicates left and pulls off, and you do like-wise. Turn to 462.

189

Those last two games have done for you. The league leaders have left you floundering in mid-table obscurity, and there's no way another three points can get you where you want to be. Trouble is, however close you might be to finding Danny, you've failed in your bid to take the title this season. So near, yet so far. Turn to 101.

190
The traffic has thinned out here, and the buildings have given way to trees as you find yourself on a dual carriageway. You have to brake sharply to stop yourself overtaking Victor, who is just up ahead and indicating left! Don't push your luck now – follow at a safe distance and turn to 462.

191
Gingerly you try the handle . . . and of course it's locked. But your chairman's obsession with the finer things in life not only includes classic cars, but also classic cars built to their original specification. There's one thing eighty grand can't buy, and that's an immobiliser alarm from 1960. Do you have a length of wire? If so, turn to 201. Otherwise you'll have to give up and return to your office (turn to 281).

192
How did your game go against Lowdham Athletic?
  If you lost to them, turn to 405.
  If the game was tied, turn to 207.
  If you beat Lowdham, turn to 337.

193
Play the match in the normal way. When you reach half-time, turn to 224.

194

Your mobile rings on your way back to the ground, so you pull over into a lay-by to answer.

'I'm sorry to bother you at the weekend,' says a familiar voice. 'This is DCI Higson. I'm calling to check if you've heard anything further about Daniel Knox's disappearance.'

Has he been watching you? What does he know? Your mind is racing.

'No, nothing,' you tell him. 'Of course I'll let you know if I do.'

'Of course you will,' the Chief Inspector says. His voice is always the same, and you can never tell what he's thinking.

'Do you have any more evidence?' you ask with genuine interest.

'Not at this moment.'

You feel particularly lonely as you end the call, and you sit for a few minutes staring out at the passing cars and wondering if anyone will ever see Danny again.

Turn to 280.

195

What a result! And away from home, those are three priceless points. So much for their legendary defence; you're obviously a natural manager. Add **1** Morale as usual for winning. The other full-time scores are available at 411.

196

The road winds ahead, and you take one turning after another. By now you're completely lost, and eventually find yourself at a dead end. You shift into reverse gear and look over your shoul-

.der, only to see a single dim headlight swing into view behind you. During the time it takes for the bullet to whistle down the length of the street, you just have time to wonder where you went wrong. It hits you between the eyes and you never find out. Turn to 101.

197
You were lucky this time! The ball wasn't struck cleanly, and it ricochets off the post and into touch. Wipe the sweat from your brow and turn to 213.

198
An excellent choice. Topflight is a very successful and popular brand, and this deal has turned out to be even better for the club than the last one. Add 2 million pounds to your Budget. Not bad for one phonecall! Now turn to 139.

199
You may continue buying and selling players if you wish. But remember you may only deal with each player once. If you haven't already, you may:

Consider selling Toby Wood?	(Turn to 282)
Consider selling Ricky Neville?	(Turn to 238)
Put in a bid for Ivan Najev?	(Turn to 464)
Put in a bid for Richard Corner?	(Turn to 251)

When you've finished changing your squad around, turn to 244.

200

Gunthorpe is a small but lively town, and it's Saturday evening so the high street is busy. Study the picture above. Any thoughts of where might be a good place to start? You may enter one of the buildings by turning to the number of that building. Alternatively you may return home by turning to 358.

201

You curl the wire into a fish-hook shape, and coax it gently down behind the door frame, glancing around furtively to make sure you're not being watched; but your only audience is a light brown whippet who is gazing at you from the back window of the car in front, head cocked comically to one side. The wire snags securely behind the locking mechanism, and as you pull the lock snaps upwards with a satisfying *thunk*. You wink at the dog and put your finger to your lips. It blinks back, uncomprehending. Turn to 401.

202
Coat, briefcase, computer – just where you left them. Maybe you should be a bit more adventurous. Go back to 107 to look at your office plan.

203
You stand up from behind the sofa and look around the now empty room again, wondering if you imagined the whole thing. Who was the meeting with in Gunthorpe? What does Victor want to keep so secret that he's hiding it in a safe at his house? And what's José Torrego got to do with all this? Carry on searching the office if you like by turning to 25. Or you could finish up for the weekend if you prefer by turning to 398.

204
Your chosen player has responded exceptionally well in training. For the rest of the season, whenever this player takes a penalty he scores automatically (make a note of this on your Fact Sheet). Remember: you can focus on two skills this week. If this was your first, turn back to 351 to choose again from the list. If you have now chosen two, turn to 430.

205
The sound of your mobile ringing startles you. It's Victor.

'Ah, there you are. Didn't you get my message? My office, five minutes.'

He hangs up before you can reply. How rude! But it could cost you your job if you refuse. Turn to 371.

206

You suggest to the linesman that he might have certain optical requirements. This really annoys him. The first time you score a goal in this match, it won't count as he will rule it offside. These are the match officials! Keep your temper in check! Now turn to 193.

207

Lowdham Athletic are unbeaten this season with two wins and a draw. Certainly an impressive record, and unfortunately better than yours. The award is duly presented to manager Bill Drebble. You send him a fax by way of congratulations, but secretly you feel a bit envious. You'll have to make some improvements in the remainder of your games if you're going to catch them. Now turn to 347.

208

Monday 14th
You wake brightly after a peaceful weekend, ready for the start of the sixth week of the league. You are first to arrive at the club, but your players soon begin filling the place with their usual noisy enthusiasm. You can hear them in the dressing room from your office, and you smile to yourself as you consider how best to channel your football expertise into their brains and boots.

What do you intend to do during the build-up towards your weekend fixture against Gunthorpe?

Focus on overall teamwork and cooperation   (Turn to 252)

Build upon tackling, containment and pressing manoeuvres
(Turn to 161)

Improve dribbling, build-up play and forward passing
(Turn to 323)

Let your assistants monitor the team's training this week
(Turn to 147)

209

The Lambley forward has found some space, and lets fly at the ball. Working on instinct, Steve Fitzgerald piles in and sticks out a desperate leg to block the shot, which has already sent your keeper the wrong way. The block takes some of the pace off the ball, but it's still spinning perilously towards the far post – exactly where Carlos de Carvalho is standing! Your two defenders have combined well and done all they can to see off this latest attack. But is it enough? Roll two dice. If you roll doubles, turn to 286. Otherwise turn to 380.

210

'You've all been pulling your weight recently, lads,' you announce to the players as they sit in the locker room pulling off muddy boots, 'and I want you to know it doesn't go unnoticed.'

'Can we have the week off then?' jokes Ant Bostock. John Hoggart hits him over the back of the head with a sweaty sock.

'No. But you can come in late tomorrow, and tonight we're having bubbly and Chinese. My treat.'

There is general excitement as the bottles are passed around and corks start whizzing through the air. But suddenly Dmitri Duval stands up and sprays a mouthful of champagne across the room.

'Zut alors! Zis is deesgusting. 'Ow am I supposed to drink zis English rubbish. It 'as all zis poudre in it.'

You grab the bottle and look. Sure enough, there is a layer of white sediment lying at the bottom.

'I feel funny, boss,' Steve Fitzgerald moans weakly.

Turn to 390.

211

You explain that you haven't seen his lucky boot, but that it must be in here somewhere. But no amount of searching reveals it, and you must now subtract **2** from Carlos's Skill for each home game you play until the boot turns up. Sometimes you feel like the tired parent of eleven children. Now turn to 215.

212

The flag goes up for a late tackle, and Bostock places the ball for a direct free kick twenty-five yards out. Jed Stevens joins the Gonalston players jockeying for position at one end of the defensive wall as Ant carefully counts six paces backwards. He begins his inimitable lope towards the ball, and you hear the usual crescendo rising from your supporters behind the goal. As his right boot connects, Jed ducks, breaking away from the wall and finding space while the defenders surge forward – and just as you'd practised, they are left in disarray by the bluff. Instead of shooting on goal, a delicate diagonal chip over the defenders pin-points Jed's head and he jumps to nod powerfully on target. Is their keeper quick enough to react?

Roll two dice: this is the Gonalston keeper's Skill. Now roll one dice and add it to Stevens's Skill. If the second number is lower, turn to 163. If it's equal or above, turn to 33.

213

The ref blows for full-time, and the game is finished. Make any necessary adjustment to the scoreline after that last little bit of excitement and turn to 414 where the rest of the day's results are coming in.

214

Play out this match in the usual way. At half-time, turn to 88.

215

Roll two dice. If you roll

2–4	(Turn to 35)
5 or 6	(Turn to 439)
7 or 8	(Turn to 449)
9–12	(Turn to 329)

216

The tyres screech as you spin the wheel and turn the car right on to Tithe Lane. Turn to 196.

217

Perhaps you have an idea about which door the key will fit.

Where do you want to try it?
Your chairman's office?	(Turn to 180)
The drying room?	(Turn to 326)
The kit room?	(Turn to 318)

218

As soon as you step into the hot, crowded room, all attention is turned to you and the flash bulbs start popping like machine-gun fire. You sit down behind the desk at the front, and reluctantly pull the microphone towards you. The questions are predictable and immediate.

'Could you comment on Danny's disappearance?' 'Have you heard anything?' 'Is it true you're having a nervous breakdown?'

'No, it's not,' you laugh. 'And one at a time please, you'll all get your turn.'

A dozen hands shoot upwards from the sea of familiar faces in the crowd. One belongs to a young woman, Anna Julian. She's one of your favourites: an ambitious journalist who sometimes asks tricky questions, but whose reporting is always professional and fair. You point to her.

'This must be a very difficult time for you and your players,' she begins sympathetically. 'Would you say that today's result was affected by Danny Knox's absence?'

How will you respond? Do you say:

'We all miss Danny around the place. That meant the other players really pulled together today, so we got exactly the result we wanted.' (Turn to 315)

or:

'Danny is a valuable member of the squad, and we'll need

more time to get used to his absence. So you've got to expect the occasional disappointment.' (Turn to 418)

219
If you haven't already done so, you may open the letter marked URGENT (turn to 3), look at the letter from the FA (turn to 394) or have a read of the local paper (turn to 172). If you wish to do none of these, turn to 89 to talk with your players.

220
Feeling sick with fear, you climb on to a chair and gingerly remove the pillowcase. Your fears are inevitably confirmed: the body belongs to Anna Julian. It's been made to look like suicide, but it can't be – she sounded so insistent on the phone. You can't bear to leave her like this, and you start unwinding the length of gardening wire binding her wrists. Her hands are still warm. And written in blue ink on her left palm are three numbers: 20–24–64. Make a note of this on your Fact Sheet. You may also keep the length of wire if you wish.

You almost fall off the chair when you hear the sound of emergency sirens and loud shouting coming from downstairs. It's the police – how did they get here so soon? And then you remember the two black-suited men who nearly charged you down on the stairs. You've been set up! Turn to 453.

221
You are well aware of how important the coming week is, and must decide how to spend your time before the next fixture. Perhaps you want to go in search of information about Danny's

whereabouts right now, in which case you should turn to 85. If you pay a visit to your ill-tempered chairman instead, turn to 371.

222

'Look, I don't know it. I mean, I've forgotten,' you falter.

'WHO IS THIS?' she hisses.

Do you explain your mistake (turn to 257) or stick to your story (turn to 426)?

223

You open the door to the women's toilets. Do you have any business here? If you're male, turn to 260. If you're female, do what you've come here to do and return to your room plan on 107.

224

Tension is high between the players as they march back to the dressing rooms at half-time. The Oxton goalkeeper makes a rude comment about Ian Leslie's mum which he takes very personally, and before you can step in a full-scale fight has broken out in the tunnel! So much for the beautiful game. But what are you going to do?

Intervene to try and sort things out?	(Turn to 137)
Wait until things settle down?	(Turn to 136)
Join in?	(Turn to 66)

225

You hand over a wad of notes, and the barman tucks them in his apron.

'I do remember them, as a matter of fact,' he tells you. 'The fat one was called Victor, the other one I can't recall. Something beginning with J. They were sat there –' he indicates the seats next to you with a nod '– didn't want to be heard.'

'And?' you enquire.

'And I didn't listen. I'm a barman, not James Bond. Now are you having a drink or what?' And he wanders over to serve somebody else.

You feel like demanding your money back but you don't want to cause a scene. As you get up to leave, the old man next to you grips your arm and pulls you back.

Turn to 109.

226

As if things couldn't get any worse, now your goalie is being shown the red card for his mistimed tackle! It's early doors for him, and he'll miss the next match. Bring on your substitute goalie. (If he is injured, put a defender in goal instead). Now turn to 58.

227

Praying there's nothing coming from either side, you change up a gear and accelerate straight over the crossroads. Safely over, you floor the accelerator. Turn to 196.

228

If you haven't already done so, you may open the letter marked URGENT (turn to 3), examine the brown parcel (turn to 316) or take a look at the *Hardwick Herald* (turn to 172). Alternatively you may go directly to speak with your players by turning to 89.

229

Seconds after the start of the second half, a lofted ball from the Lambley anchorman falls to the feet of their attacking midfielder, and he makes a dangerous run into your six-yard box. Are you playing the defensive combination of Fitzgerald and de Carvalho? If so, turn to 209. Otherwise turn to 442.

230

The betting shop is half-empty, and the cashiers look bored. There are a couple of screens in one corner showing slow-motion replays of greyhounds and a horse race about to start. You put a bet on one of the horses and it comes last. The manager laughs when you ask her if she's seen anything suspicious on the premises, and she laughs.

'In 'ere? All the time, love. Why do you think we got these bandit-screens up?' She taps the bullet-proof glass between you both with a long painted fingernail.

You decide not to waste any more time and return home for the evening. Turn to 358.

231

Jamie went the right way – but the ball was just too high for him. It clears his outstretched mitt by a couple of inches, and flies into the stanchion for a goal. Sadly for you, a perfect penalty will always beat perfect goalkeeping. Now turn to 213.

232

Saturday 19th

Early on the morning of your match you drive to the club, where the team will soon be congregating. You always like to travel to these away fixtures in the official bus with the players themselves, to create a feeling of solidarity. Your chairman, however – when he goes at all, that is – prefers the comfortable isolation of his Jaguar. He's just leaving as you arrive, and your cars pass in the wide gateway of the club grounds.

'Off to the match already, Victor?' you ask him.

'Not today. I'm away for the weekend.'

Typical to be skipping a match – he generally prefers a long game of golf followed by an even longer gin and tonic. But odd that he tried to slip away without telling you.

'Have a safe journey,' you say brightly, but his dark window is already up, and anyway the players have started to arrive. Turn to 54.

233

If your deepest defenders run forward at exactly the right moment, an opposition striker can be forced offside. It requires great cooperation and timing, but when the offside trap is employed properly it can be a great defensive manoeuvre. Choose a Defender to be in charge of the offside trap. Now roll one dice. If you roll 1–4, turn to 44. If you roll 5 or 6, turn to 404.

234

Back in the dressing room after the match, Fitzgerald is still red-faced and fuming. How will you deal with this? If you take him to one side and give him a sharp telling-off, turn to 336. If you think it's better to ignore it and leave him to calm down, turn to 97.

235

'You've worked hard all week,' you eulogise, 'and today you can reap your rewards. You know me well by now: it's goals I've brought you here for, and it's goals I want.'

You draw a picture of a goal on the blackboard to emphasise your point, and your attackers nod in unison.

'I've set out my stall. And all I'm selling is three points. Do I have any buyers?'

Your team chorus their approval, and look focused. Jed Stevens is still staring hard at the blackboard. You may add **1** to the Skill of any two of your Attackers for this match. Now play it out in the usual way, and when you reach the 30th minute turn to 75.

236

You climb one flight and knock on the heavy oak door marked Chairman. But when you enter, you are surprised to discover he is not alone. Two constables are sitting on the other side of his desk, and they stand as you close the door behind you.

'What's happened?' you ask. 'Is there any news about Danny?'

'In a manner of speaking,' replies one of the policemen. 'A short while ago we had a call from a Mr Vivian Sprike – says he's got information linking you to the abduction of Mr Knox.'

'Me?' you splutter. 'I – no, this is wrong. It's just sour grapes because I fired him.'

'We have to investigate everything in a matter of this gravity,' the other policeman says.

'You do understand I must consider the good of my club,' Victor tells you in a patronising tone. 'Of course when this is all cleared up you can come back to your job, but for now I'm afraid . . .' He tails off, but you understand only too well.

'If you wouldn't mind,' the first constable says, indicating the door. And as they lead you out of the office, you look back to see Victor's mouth broaden into a glistening smile.

Turn to 101.

237

'They say football is all about scoring goals, and that's never been truer than in this exciting fixture between two in-form teams. Let's go over to Hardwick's home ground where they're about to kick off.'

Here's a reminder of how to calculate your Match Factor.

First, work out your team's Overall Skill by adding up the Skills of your chosen players. Write it in the box on your Match Sheet.

As you just saw on the Team Profile, Lowdham's Overall Skill is 66. Write this in too.

Next, put in your Morale and Fitness.

Remember to add 3 because you're playing at your home ground, and there's your Match Factor. When you're ready, turn to 55.

238

You're the boss: and if you think Ricky Neville is too much of a liability at the back you can get rid of him. But how much money will he command on the open market? Roll one dice, and subtract it from Ricky's Skill. That's how many millions Woodborough will offer you for his talents. Let Mr Neville walk if the money talks: remember to remove his name from your Fact Sheet and add this new cash to your Budget. If the number is zero or less, you just can't come to an agreement and the deal's off.

When you're ready, turn to 199 to decide what to do next.

239

The fourth official raises his electronic signboard. Four added minutes of injury time! Where on earth did that come from? In such a finely-balanced match, anything could happen. Roll one dice. If you roll 1–3, turn to 148. If you roll 4 or more, turn to 16. If you are playing the strong midfield combination of Hurley and Wehnert, you may add **1** to the dice roll.

240

Your chosen player has responded exceptionally well in training. For the rest of the season, you may add **2** to the dice roll whenever this player takes a free kick (make a note of this on your Fact Sheet). Remember: you can focus on two skills this week. If this was your first, turn back to 351 to choose again from the list. If you have now chosen two, turn to 430.

241

You punch the number into the phone, and after three rings a receptionist answers.

'The Ship Hotel, can I help
you?'

'Room 209 please.'

There is a brief pause while
you are connected, then the
phone begins to ring again.

You are startled at how quickly it is answered, and the voice on
the other end is female. Turn to 428.

242

You begin sifting through the piles of paper on the bed. Most of
it is junk, empty files, old newspapers. You look under the bed,
behind the chest of drawers, you even stand on a chair to look
on top of the wardrobes, but whoever was here before you did a
very thorough job. Be careful not to touch anything that might
leave fingerprints. Do you want to examine the body? If so, turn
to 220. If you'd rather get out of here, turn to 453.

243

You jump out of the car. The man who followed you here from
your club is lying unconscious and face-down on the tarmac,
hands cuffed behind his back. Your mysterious ally removes its
gas-mask, and you see behind it a gaunt but familiar face.

'Vivian Sprike, ex-Special Forces. Hello, chief.'

'Oh my God. You saved my life.'

'I saved up a few bits of kit too,' he smiles, nodding at the
empty gas canister. 'After I was injured on a training mission I
had to leave the brigade.'

'I never knew,' you tell him honestly.

'You never asked.' His voice is stern but his face is cordial, and you feel a wave of guilt as you realise you've known him for ages but never talked to him.

'But how did you know where to come?'

'I didn't. You worked that out. The rest was easy: they followed you, and I followed them. Time to finish operation Danny Boy, don't you think?'

You nod, and the two of you walk over to Unit 29.

Turn to 29.

244

You're determined to manage your team to an important home win this coming Saturday against Woodborough County. You walk to the dressing room expecting to find it empty so early in the day, but Ian Leslie has beaten you to it this morning. Look back over your matches so far this season. How many times have you played Ian Leslie in your line-up?

0–2 times?　　　　(Turn to 26)
3 times?　　　　　(Turn to 295)
4 or more times?　(Turn to 12)

245

You run over to the sofa and dive quickly behind it, trying to steady your breathing so as not to give yourself away. But whoever has come in seems not to have seen you, and you hear footsteps pad over to the cabinet. A jacket flops over the back of the sofa, and its fabric dangles inches from your face. You can see the tips of polished brogues at eye-level, and you hear the clink of bottle on glass as the sour smell of whisky hits your nose. You daren't move a muscle. The feet disappear and pad softly in the direction of the desk, and your unwelcome guest starts humming gently to himself. He sounds disturbingly contented, but thankfully quite unaware of your presence as he picks up the receiver to his desk phone and taps in a number. Better stay where you are and turn to 178.

246

'Yes, it's Sam,' you lie, trying to sound confident. 'I'm phoning to see if you've got any information on Danny Knox.'

'Sam? Sam who?' she asks nervously. 'I don't know you. If you're from *Newsdesk* you'll know the code I gave you.'

Help! Do you know the code? If so, turn to that number. If not, turn to 222.

247

You pick up one of the larger pebbles from the driveway, weigh it up in your hand, and take aim. The stone smashes cleanly and almost noiselessly through the glass. Unfortunately the house is alarmed. Roll one dice. If you roll 1–4, turn to 340. If you roll 5 or 6, turn to 141.

248

You close the safe door and give the wheel a couple of spins before leaving silently the way you came. The street is deserted – lucky for you it's the kind of place where everyone keeps to themselves. Back on the main road you flag down a black cab and within half an hour you're back in your office. Your hands are shaking as you fire up your computer and insert the CD-ROM. The disk contains two files: a word-processing document and a spreadsheet. You open up both of them, and as you begin to read everything starts to fall into place.

Turn to 250.

249

The penny drops. Of course: the initials JT, the moustache, the planned attacks on the other managers. That only leaves Jack Tatchell. You jump in your car, and gun the engine. Oxton's less than fifty miles away – you can get there in under an hour. The tyres screech as you pull out of the car park and on to the main road. It's dark now. You have seen that the lights up ahead are green, and you lean on the accelerator. What you haven't seen is that a black saloon with two men inside has pulled away from the kerb where they were waiting for you. The car tails you at a respectable distance, and forty-five minutes later you've pulled into a lay-by on the Oxton approach. Turn to 19.

250

The spreadsheet contains a lot of numeric data, but it's obviously a set of accounts. There are details of money coming in, money going out – lots of it, millions of pounds – along with bank account details. You recognise one bank account as being that of Hardwick City FC.

The other document is even more revealing. The first section contains dates of transactions between a number of internet bookmakers and two individuals, identified only by their initials: VS and JT. The first must be Victor, the second – well, maybe you've got your suspicions. All bets are football bets, and each is for between fifty and a hundred thousand pounds. That's shady enough. But the second section almost stops your heart.

Sat 8th. Take care of Danny Knox. Location as agreed. Drug players if Hardwick still doing too well.

If the following teams threaten our position in league:

Sat 29th. Have the boys pay Gonalston players a friendly visit

Fri 18th. Bomb scare at Woodborough

When you've digested this data, turn to 138.

251

If you want to buy this defender you'll have to decide how many millions you're going to offer. Then roll one dice and add it to your bid. Is this number bigger than Corner's Skill of 5? If it is, you've got yourself a new team member! Add his name to your Fact Sheet and don't forget to deduct the money you spend from your Budget. If the number is equal or lower, you've been refused.

You only get one try at this! When you've finished wheeling and dealing, turn to 199.

252

If you wish to concentrate on the team as a whole, turn to 279. If you single out certain players for praise, turn to 38.

253

On the bus on your way back home, you tell your players you're disappointed with their behaviour in the tunnel.

'They started it,' Ricky Neville protests.

'Everybody is having to grow up,' shouts Klaus Wehnert, sensibly.

'But if it's your family name it is personal,' Carlos de Carvalho mutters.

'Stick to the football!' you insist. 'Do you want to win this league or not?'

But as the players joke and tease each other, your mind is already on other things. Do you have an address you wish to investigate? If so, add together the room number and the street number and turn to that paragraph. If not, you eventually arrive back at your office. Turn to 280.

254

You are making your way back to the team coach when your secretary phones you. It's not good news. Right at this moment, a letter is being typed. When you arrive back at your office, it will be signed, sealed and waiting for you on your desk. When you open it, you will see that it has been written on official Hardwick City notepaper. When you finish reading the letter you will slump into your chair, deflated; because the letter tells you that your performance has been 'less than satisfactory', and that your career at this football club is over. It's signed, of course, on behalf of the board, by a certain V. Sinkowski.

Danny won't make it home now: whoever kidnapped him has beaten you. Your adventure is over this time. Turn to 101.

255

You run to the locker room and fling open the door.

'What's going on?' you demand.

All the players have arrived and are getting changed. They are laughing and jeering at Carlos de Carvalho, who is running around wearing one red boot and a worried look.

'Ma shoe, I cannot play without ma shoe,' he shouts.

'He hasn't seen it for two weeks,' Will Frost chimes in helpfully above the laughter.

So Carlos has lost his lucky boot. 'Can't you wear the ones you had on last Saturday?' you ask wearily.

'Don't be crazy. They away shoes. This *home* shoe.'

Trust fashion-conscious Carlos to have home and away boots. But superstition can be a powerful thing with some athletes. Do you have his lucky red boot? If so, turn to 365. If not, turn to 211.

256

Roll for this free kick in the usual way (where 5 or 6 = Goal), then continue with the match until its conclusion. When the 90 minutes are up, turn to 377.

257

'Look, you don't know me,' you explain, giving your name. 'I'm the manager at Hardwick City. There have been some strange things happening here since Danny disappeared and I came across this address.'

There is a long, chilling pause.

'I do know you, actually,' she says. 'This is Anna Julian – I interviewed you last Saturday after the match, remember?'

'Of course – but –' You falter, relieved to hear a friendly voice, but more confused than ever. 'What's going on? What are you doing there?'

'I think I'm on to something about Danny Knox. But they must have found me,' she whispers, almost to herself. 'This line might be bugged. And anyway, how do I know you are who you say you are?'

'I can come and meet you,' you suggest.

'OK, but hurry. We may not have much time. And come alone.'

Your car keys are in your pocket. What are you waiting for? Turn to 459 to follow this new lead. Or is it a trap? Err on the side of caution by turning to 280.

258

As quick as a rat out of a trap, your keeper drops to the ground and blocks the ball. Your defenders do the rest, and the ball is cleared to safety. After you've opened your eyes, complete the second half in the normal way. Then turn to 319.

259

Turn to 165.

260

What are you doing? You feel you don't belong here. The sound of a toilet flushing means you leave in a hurry; return to 107 and your room plan.

261

SureTech seem very eager to get the publicity, and agree to the deal. Make a note on your Fact Sheet of your new sponsor's name, and turn to 175.

262

You stay late in your office this evening, long after everyone has gone home for the night. You sift through the clues you've gathered along the way, wondering if they could lead you to Danny's whereabouts. Now's the time to put the jigsaw together; and if you've followed the correct path through this book, you will now know which manager is behind all this and where Danny Knox is being held captive. Detective-manager, once again you are faced with a choice. Whose home town will you visit?

Jules Torrence	(Turn to 46)
Jake Tapper	(Turn to 307)
Bill Drebble	(Turn to 259)
Jack Tatchell	(Turn to 249)
José Torrego	(Turn to 368)

263

Chilling. You place the weapon back where you found it and click shut the compartment. Have you looked through Victor's jacket pockets yet? If not you may do so by turning to 290. Otherwise head back to your office and turn to 281 when you get there.

264

Toby has been eagerly anticipating this fixture for some time. He's anxious to impress his new manager Eric Redman, and wants to show you that you made the wrong choice in selling him to your rivals. He will play in the middle of their attacking line-up for this match, so you must add a further **3** to Lambley's Overall Skill. Turn to 50.

265

If your team were stronger and fitter, they would recover better from injuries. You decide to spend the week concentrating on circuit training and gym work. See how your squad responds by rolling one dice.

If you roll 1, 2 or 3, add **1** to your team's Fitness.
If you roll 4, 5 or 6, add **2** to your team's Fitness.
Got your breath back? Turn to 419.

266

Subtract **2** from your dice roll. Ian Leslie is getting nervous with all the pressure. Turn to 348.

267

You'll have to think on your feet. What are you going to do? If you hide behind the sofa, turn to 245. If you confront whoever's letting themselves in, turn to 17.

268

You are unable to shift the base of the locker and must eventually give up. It's probably empty anyway. Now return to your room plan and decide where to visit next.

269

Friday 23rd
You're amazed at how fast these things make the press. Within forty-eight hours all the papers were leading with the story, with varying degrees of accuracy. All, however, agreed that Danny

wouldn't be alive today if not for the unlikely manager/kit man pairing of you and Vivian Sprike.

That was three weeks ago. You submitted the CD-ROM and the notes you found to police forensics. Victor Sinkowski and Jack Tatchell are currently in police custody without bail, awaiting sentences for (among other things) assault, conspiracy and misappropriation of club funds. DCI Higson – remember him? – took a statement from you that lasted most of the day. The junior officers were all eager to meet you after the story of Danny's rescue leaked out, but Higson had been stern.

'You should have told us,' he had cautioned gruffly. But his face had been gentle and reassuring, and he'd treated you kindly.

Danny's been the big centre of attention, of course. He passed a medical with flying colours, and the experts have been falling over each other to give their opinions on the local news. 'He's at home with his wife and we expect him to make a full recovery,' seems to be the official line.

As for the football, the FA put paid to wild newspaper speculation by quickly issuing the following statement.

'In light of recent events, Oxton Wanderers will be disqualified this season. We apologise to the club's innocent supporters and players. The final matches of the season will be postponed for a fortnight, and will now take place on Saturday 24th. We ask all clubs to be undeterred and patient during this time.'

That's tomorrow afternoon. You've spent as much time as possible with your players in the last three weeks, and as you sit at home this Friday evening you smile to yourself at just how well-behaved they've been for you. You're just about to go to bed when the phone rings.

'It's me, Danny. I've been thinking. I know they've told me to take the rest of the season off, but I'm feeling OK, you know. I've been exercising, I've put some weight back on – look, it's your call, but what about giving me a game tomorrow?'

'I'm not sure that's such a good idea, Dan,' you say cautiously, but inside your heart is brimming at the thought of watching your flagship striker play for Hardwick again. You don't take much persuading. 'First sign of fatigue I'm taking you off,' you warn him.

Danny's grin is audible. 'Thanks, boss. See you bright and early.'

Turn to 443.

270

Your goalie flings himself at the feet of the forward as he brings back his boot to kick the ball. It is smothered before he can connect, and his momentum takes him harmlessly over the top of your prone goalkeeper who is hugging the ball close. Brave keeping, and he's saved some red faces after that defensive error. Turn to 80.

271

Your defence is having all sorts of problems out there. The Lambley forwards are piling on the pressure, and crosses are flying in from both flanks. Subtract **3** from your Match Factor for this game. Now turn to 376.

272

Look back over your five Match Sheets. Of all the players in your squad, are there any players who haven't played in a single match so far? If there is anyone you haven't tried out, turn to 285. If everyone has had a go – even if it's just as a sub – turn to 331.

273

'I'll come help if I can.'

Those were Viv Sprike's last words to you when he gave you that bleeper, and if you ever needed help it's now. You take it from your pocket and press the button repeatedly, all the while watching behind you as the saloon gets closer and closer. In your rear-view mirror, stage-lit by two dozen security lights, you have a perfect view of what happens next. The saloon comes to a stop, and you hear the ratchet of the handbrake being pulled. The driver's door opens, and the man whose job it is to kill you steps out. He stands there for a few seconds, motionless, and you feel the cold thrill of fear at the nape of your neck. The last thing you expect to see is a figure with a long snout scurry behind the saloon from one side to the other. It's so quick and silent you wonder if you imagined it. The man appears to be in no hurry, and you watch him pulling off his gloves when you hear a soft clink-clink-clink of metal against tarmac. He pauses, glove half-off, and looks down at his feet. Then he disappears completely behind clouds of white smoke which billow and glow against the floodlit street. You spin round in your seat, and when the smoke clears moments later, your would-be assassin has gone. In his place, standing perfectly still and straight, is the snouted figure. Turn to 243.

274

Turning the night's events over in your mind, you can hardly sleep. You want to go to the police, but you'd never forgive yourself if Danny came to any harm. 'He thinks he can win the league,' Danny had said. So it's one of the other managers who's at the centre of this! They're all listed back on page 24, and at the moment every one of them is on your list of suspects. But which of them has come up with this evil scheme?

You sleep fitfully, and wake early on Saturday morning. Turn to 131.

275

Saturday 26th

The week's training has gone well and your players are eager to give Woodborough a thrashing. The atmosphere in the dressing room is tense but positive, and you can hear the expectant hum of supporters packing your home ground. Take a look at the competition this week:

Woodborough County FC
Overall Skill: 68

Jose Torrego has taken Woodborough to some convincing victories this season already, and they're looking good despite recent events. But they're strongest at home, and you should be able to turn over a team like this if you're going to finish at the top of the table.

At 2:30, you gather your squad around you before letting them on to the pitch to warm up. Do you wish to place the emphasis on attack (turn to 235) or on defence (turn to 140)?

276

You swing left and find yourself on open road. Turn to 105.

277

Half-time in a home game, and you feel you ought to be winning. This wasn't the plan; your players look tired, and their morale is beginning to wane. Do you decide to give them a half-time pep-talk to lift their spirits? If so, turn to 386. If you think they can turn things around in the second half, turn to 448.

278

Are you winning? If so, turn to 448. If you are behind or drawing level, turn to 277.

279

The raucous dressing room is full when you walk in, but your squad settles down respectfully as their commander stands in the centre of the room.

'You all make significant individual contributions to this squad,' you begin telling them with conviction, 'but the whole is greater than the sum of its parts.'

Roll one dice. If you roll 1, turn to 151. If you roll 2–6 turn to 130.

280

Monday 24th

You arrive at your office before your players are due to turn up for training, and spend an hour or so drinking coffee and reading the press. This used to be such a quiet city. Now the headlines are full of things like 'SureTech Phones: Share Price Tumbles', 'Reporter Found Dead In Hotel Room – Police Suspect Foul Play' and 'Pet Shop Trashed By Furious Monkeys'. Is there any good news these days? With a sigh you turn your attention to next Saturday's home fixture against Papplewick Town. But before you have time to think about your strategy, you hear shouting from the locker room. Turn to 255.

281

You're back in your office after a tiring afternoon. Who is the current sponsor of Hardwick City?

SureTech Phones?	(Turn to 49)
Topflight Sportswear?	(Turn to 198)
Don't know?	(Turn to 306)

282

How does Woody fit into your spearhead these days? Perhaps you like a bit of healthy competition among your strikers, as it keeps them goal-hungry and keen to impress you. Maybe he's the hub of your strike force and you'd rather manage a netball team than lose him to your rivals. Or maybe you're already packing his bags and thinking about what you can do with the transfer fee. As always, it's up to you.

If you'd like to see what you can get for your striker, roll one dice and subtract it from Toby's Skill. This is the number of millions Lambley Rovers are prepared to pay. If you want to accept their offer, remove Mr Wood from your Fact Sheet and add the money to your Budget. If the number was zero or less, I'm afraid they've lost interest.

You can only try this once! When you've finished these negoti-ations, turn to 199.

283

You might not be out of the woods just yet, but you're still in the hat for a chance at winning this league! Keep your eyes focused on the job ahead, because there's still work to do in this book – there's the small matter of getting Danny Knox back safe and sound for a start. Now get back on the coach and talk over the match with your players as you make your way back to Hardwick City FC. Turn to 437.

284

The envelope feels heavy in your hands, and as you open it a small silver key falls out. There's a note attached, written in a clear hand:

You smile inwardly as you pocket the key. Perhaps you can guess who it's from. But there's no time for investigation now – there's a football match to play. Turn to 11.

285

No one joins a football club just to sit around. Any player who hasn't yet played in a match loses **1** point from his Skill. Turn to 331.

286

Oh dear. Double means trouble, and despite de Carvalho's every effort, he can't divert the ball from its course. It flies past him into the back of the net, to the joy of the opposition fans. Add 1 to the Lambley score, gather your wits, and play out the rest of the second half. When the fat lady sings, you can turn to 319.

287

The first away game, and your constant snooping has meant your players are far from the polished and disciplined fighting force you had intended. Lose **1** Fitness and **1** Morale, and subtract **1** from the Skill of any five of your players for the duration of this next match. Remember you've got a job to do as well as a crime to solve. Oh, it's too late for excuses. Turn to 350.

288

Over the roundabout you continue to drive at speed through the outskirts of the city, the Little Elvis hanging from your windscreen gyrating wildly. After a minute you reach another roundabout, this time with two exits. Do you take the one to the left (turn to 190) or the right (turn to 126)?

289

Monday 21st

You arrive on Monday morning to a flurry of administrative activity. With three matches to go until the end of the season and all teams jockeying for position in the league table, the transfer market has been flooded with requests for players to be bought and sold. The first thing you notice is that Lambley Rovers have made a huge pre-emptive offer of 10 million to secure the services of top Brazilian winger Sheldinho. That's a shame – he could have brought some width to Hardwick's attack. Are you interested in seeing which other players are on the move? If so, turn to 118. If not, turn to 244.

290

In one pocket is a Havana cigar, still in its metal sheath. In the other is a neatly folded piece of cream notepaper with writing on it. Better not start smoking – your health is already at risk just by being in this car. But you can read the notepaper if you wish by turning to 359. If you'd prefer to search the glove box, and haven't already done so, turn to 82. If you think you should get back to your office while you've still time, turn to 281.

291

Are you playing the combination of Bobak, Hoggart and Wood? If so, turn to 111. Otherwise, follow the match to its conclusion then turn to 397.

292

You plunge forward, full steam ahead on to Neville Close. Turn to 196.

293

One point to each team – a tight result in a closely fought game. Your position in the league now depends on the rest of the results, which are coming in on 402.

294

During the training period you are struck by the understanding that has developed between Masashi Suda and Salvatore Duce. They are cooperating well on the pitch, monitoring each other's position and feeding balls unselfishly to set up goal opportunities. Strikers so often want to work alone, and it's rare to see two pairing up so well together. Masashi was a good buy. From now on, you may add **1** to the Skill of each player whenever they play together in a match. Now turn to 275.

295

Your striker stands up as you enter the dressing room, but his expression is not happy.

'I need to talk to you,' he tells you firmly. 'You don't seem to want me here as a player. I've only played in half the matches so far and I know I'm better than that. I need to know if you're going to put me in for ninety minutes this weekend.'

Ian is an ambitious individual and it looks like he's getting restless. What do you tell him? Are you going to give him the exposure he wants (turn to 375)? Or do you tell him he will have to be patient (turn to 143)?

296

Epperstone Town want 5 million pounds for Masashi Suda. Do you want him? If you do, here are the rules for buying a player. First, decide how many millions you're willing to pay. Next, roll one dice and add the number to your offer.

If this total is **higher** than Masashi's asking price (5 in this case), your offer is accepted! Add Masashi's name to your squad, and deduct the payment from your Budget. But if it's equal or lower you've been refused. You only get one go at this, so decide carefully how much you'd like to offer.

When you've finished, turn to 454.

297

So, you've played six matches now which means you're two-thirds of the way through your campaign. How are you faring in the league? Do you have

Less than 7 points?   (Turn to 254)
7 to 13 points?   (Turn to 283)
14 points or more?   (Turn to 429)

298

For the next match only, add **2** to the Skill of any two of your Defenders but subtract **1** from each of your Attackers. Turn to 6.

299

You carefully tear back the heavy-duty brown paper. Underneath is a label saying 'Dollinger 1989'. That's a good champagne! You remove the case from its wrapping, and read the card inside. 'Keep up the good work! From all at Hardwick City FC.' How nice – your staff are so thoughtful. If you treat yourself to a quick tipple now, turn to 164. If you really ought to save it to drink later with your players, turn to 219.

300
It's late now, you're tired and can't think straight, and tomorrow's a big day. You turn round in the direction of home.
Turn to 274.

301
Ten minutes of the interval left and the clock's ticking. The three of you are standing there in an awkward silence. Your move: are you going to try to cajole them and make them see reason? If so turn to 406. If you'd rather come down on them like a ton of bricks turn to 333.

302
Roll one dice. If you roll 1–4 turn to 13. If you roll 5 or 6 turn to 281.

303
You move to pick up one of the books, but it doesn't budge. It's joined to all the other books and they're all made of plastic! What a faker. The façade swings up on hinges to reveal the real contents of the cabinet – very old, very fine whisky and port. What does the old soak do up here all day? But there's no time to won-

der as you hear the sound of a key being turned in the lock behind you. Shut the cabinet door and turn to 267.

304
Your defence is under siege but manages to hold up well while the game settles down. Turn to 376.

305
'Can you hear me?'

'I think he's drunk,' you hear a familiar voice saying. It's Ian Leslie.

'Bleurgh,' you manage.

'Look at this bottle,' Ant Bostock is saying. 'There's all white stuff in the bottom.'

You've been spiked!

'The staff gave it to me,' you tell them.

'We don't know anything about it,' your secretary protests. 'It was delivered this morning.'

'Better get you home to bed, chief,' Will Frost says.

You spend the week recovering. Lose **2** Morale for scaring your team and **2** Fitness as you're not around to coach them this week. Now turn to 48.

306

There was an important letter that you really should have opened last week. You didn't, and now the club's funds have dwindled to nothing under your very nose. Change your Budget to zero, and subtract **2** Morale as the future of Hardwick City is now uncertain. Turn to 139.

307

Turn to 165.

308

You settle in your seat in the dugout, and begin to feel that familiar surge of adrenalin and pride as your team files past you to the deafening roar of thousands of your fans. While the players are warming up, one of the ball-girls runs up to you, wearing an immaculate miniature Hardwick City strip. She chews her lip nervously, then thrusts an envelope towards you.

'I've been told to give you this. Says it's important.'

She beams at you then trots away before you can ask who gave her these instructions. Do you open the envelope (turn to 284) or ignore it (turn to 11)?

309

There's nothing here. Do you stubbornly continue searching under the flowerpots (turn to 96), smash a window (turn to 247) or try the garage door (turn to 187)?

310

For this match only you may add **1** to the Skill of each of your

Attackers. Now turn to 237 to play your first match!

311

It's a .45 revolver – make a note of this number on your Fact Sheet for later. You pop open the cylinder and shake out six bullets into the palm of your hand. They're real, all right. You place the gun exactly back where you found it and close the compartment. If you've not yet done so you may rifle through the pockets of Victor's jacket by turning to 290. Otherwise turn to 281 to hot-foot it back to your office.

312

You gingerly swing open the metal door, and peer inside. You are surprised to find it empty, and somehow you doubt Danny left it this way. You are about to close it and leave, but something makes you stop. The floor of the locker is made of a slightly different colour metal to the rest. A false bottom – you try to prise it up with your fingers but it's jammed in. Do you have anything to prise it open with? If you have found a steel letter-opener, turn to 345. If not, turn to 354.

313

Your chosen player has responded well in training. For the rest of the season, you may add **1** to the dice roll whenever this player takes a penalty (make a note of this on your Fact Sheet). Remember: you can focus on two skills this week. If this was your first, turn back to 351 to choose again from the list. If you have now chosen two, turn to 430.

314

You ask around but it seems the town is full of hotels and you don't know which one to visit. You're wasting your time – go back home and turn to 358.

315

Did you win today? If so, turn to 104. If not, turn to 2.

316

The package is large, about the size of a milk crate, and it is addressed to you in thick black handwriting. There is no stamp. Will you open it (turn to 299), or ignore it (turn to 219)?

317

Dmitri Duval reacts quickly to the defensive error and begins a sprint towards the Bridgford attacker. Ricky Neville sees exactly what is about to happen, and drops into a containing position to cover the route to goal. Duval throws himself into a sliding tackle with expert timing, disarming the forward and leaving the ball loose for Neville to collect. It's a great tackle, but the Bridgford player decides to fall over and appeal for the free kick. Ah, it's a sad thing that all the old-fashioned values have been squeezed out of the modern game. But how gullible is the referee? Roll two dice. If you roll doubles, turn to 434, otherwise turn to 57.

318

You leave your office and walk up the corridor to the right. The kit-room door is shut, and you can see from under the door that there is no light on inside. Are you sure about this? If so, turn to

110. If you'd prefer to try a different room, go back to 217 and choose again.

319
Here are the rest of the day's results.

```
   Bridgford City 3 — 3 Papplewick Town
  Epperstone Town 2 — 0 Woodborough County
  Gonalston City 0 — 2 Oxton Wanderers
Lowdham Athletic 1 — 1 Gunthorpe Utd
```

Fill in a new League Table, and turn to 158.

320
The free kick is taken but your strong defence crowds out the attack in the box. Finally a poorly sliced half-volley goes well wide of the back post. This to the obvious relief of your home fans who express themselves with colourful adjectives and arms held wide. Seconds after the restart the ref blows to wrap up the match. Turn to 234.

321
Choose a team member to be your penalty-taker. Now roll one dice. If you roll 1–3, turn to 204. If you roll 4–6, turn to 313.

322
For the next match only, add **1** to the Skill of any two of your Defenders. Turn to 6.

323

'When you go to Gunthorpe for dinner,' you begin, 'you never know what's going to be on the menu.'

'I'll be cooking goal pie!' Ben Parker tells you eagerly.

'I'll be carving up the defence,' adds John Hoggart.

'Und I vill be making deep crosses into ze box,' says Klaus Wehnert, missing the joke.

'I hope so,' you tell them encouragingly, 'but I urge caution. Gunthorpe aren't a team to just sit down and walk away. They're in front of their own fans, and they're going to make you dig deep. I'm going to make sure you've got big pockets.'

Roll one dice. If you roll 1–5, turn to 116. If you roll 6, turn to 445.

324

Gunthorpe United are asking 6 million for Jonny Steel. Is he worth it? Here's how it works. If you want to buy him, decide how many millions you're willing to pay. Now roll one dice and add the number to your offer.

If this total is **more** than his asking price (6 in this case) your bid has been accepted! Welcome him to your squad and add his name on your Fact Sheet. But if the number is equal or lower, your offer is refused. You only get one chance at this, so decide carefully – and remember you can't offer more money than you've actually got!

When you've finished, turn to 454.

325

Jonny Steel and Ricky Neville approach you before the training week begins.

'Just thought you'd like to know we've settled our differences,' Neville says.

'Glad to hear it,' you tell them both warmly.

Restore their Skills to their former values before they fell out. Now turn to 34.

326
You make your way through the damp heat of the laundry room and push the key into the lock of the drying-room door. It fits! But it doesn't turn. It's the wrong key, and now it's stuck fast. You twist and shout but it won't come out. Eventually it snaps in the lock and there's nothing more you can do. Turn to 398.

327
You keep the car on a course dead ahead. The crossroads flashes by as you enter Spindle View. Turn to 196.

328
The Papplewick keeper is braced against the goalmouth, gloved hands held wide. Sixty thousand pairs of eyes are trained on the ball just twelve yards in front of him. The ball is struck cleanly . . . Roll two dice and make a note of your roll. Who is taking this penalty?

Duce?	(Turn to 122)
Leslie?	(Turn to 266)
Someone else?	(Turn to 348)

329
Your front three are doing just what you pay them to do in training this week. They are moving fast in the box, anticipating well,

and their shooting is accurate and sure. Add **1** to the Skill of any <u>two</u> of your Attackers for this match only. Now turn to 421.

330
You open the door to the men's toilets. Do you have any business here? If you're female, turn to 260. If you're male, do what you've come here to do and return to your room plan on 107.

331
Another day, another match notched up. You stick around to thank your players for their hard work today and to make sure the place is in order. The rest of the staff are away and all the executives seem to have long gone. You're alone in your own club – just the way you like it. Are you in possession of a silver key? If so, turn to 370. If not turn to 398.

332
You swing the car round to the right on to another desolate street. Turn to 196.

333
'I've just about had enough of this!' you roar. The players flinch, but you continue. 'I don't know what this is about and I don't care. But I'm telling you –' here you lower your voice for maximum effect '– any more of this and you'll take no part in this match at all. Clear?'

Neville and Steel look at each other, then at you.

'I SAID IS THAT CLEAR?' you bellow.

'Do what you like, boss,' Jonny mutters.

'I'm not playing with that loser,' Ricky asserts.

Now you've done it. Worse still, to retain any kind of credibility you'll have to stick to your word. If either was playing in the first half, you must substitute him. If you don't have enough defenders you'll have to bring on someone else, remembering to subtract **2** from their Skill for playing in an unnatural role. What a pity. Sometimes players just clash, and maybe next time a softer approach might work a bit better. If you play Jonny Steel and Ricky Neville together again in future you must deduct **2** from each player's Skill for their non-cooperation. Subtract **1** Morale for all the unpleasantness, and turn to 60.

334

For the next match only, add **2** to the Skill of any two of your Attackers. Turn to 6.

335

'Work hard for me this week,' you tell your squad, 'and I'll take you all to Alton Towers on Thursday. Mess around and we're going to the cinema. To watch foreign films.'

'What – with all writing at the bottom?' asks Jamie Coates, gloomily.

'Subtitles, you pillock,' says John Hoggart.

Jamie begins his training immediately and the rest of the team follow suit. They work hard and you give them their day out: you may add **1** Morale and **2** Fitness as a result.

Turn to 344.

336

'Would you like to tell me what the hell you think you're playing at?' you snap when you get him alone.

'What? You saw – I didn't do anything. Why should I get punished on a 50-50 ball?' Steve protests breathlessly.

'Didn't do anything?' You cock your head and glare at him. 'You got yourself carded – is that what you think you're paid for? Maybe it was a poor decision, maybe not – but once the ref's made his mind up you shut your mouth and get on with it. This is a professional team, not a Sunday league for frustrated estate agents. When you're on the field you represent me and you represent your team. Don't let me down like that again.'

Steve Fitzgerald has nothing to say and returns to his locker where he sits and tugs furiously at his boot laces. He's angry now, but you were right and he knows it – he was stupid to act all macho like that and needs to learn a little humility. Leave him be now – later he'll apologise for his behaviour. Hey – good management! Now turn to 129.

337

Gunthorpe United are flying high with two wins and a draw, and the MotM award is rightly presented to manager Jake Tapper. His smug grin will surely be all over the back pages tomorrow. Bad luck or bad management, it could have been you; but that's life. Now pick yourself up and get back in the race on paragraph 347.

338

For the next match only, add **2** to the Skill of any two of your Midfielders. Now turn to 6.

339

Back in your office, you place together the scrap of paper you found in the kidnapper's wallet and the one that fell out of the map. Together they make a complete page. But why was one of them in Victor's office? You decide to investigate, and look up the address on the internet. There it is, The Ship Hotel, Taylor Street. It's about 30 minutes from here by car, but maybe you should telephone first. To dial the number, turn to 241. To forget the whole thing, turn to 280.

340

You were lucky this time – the stone wasn't enough to set off the alarm. Unfortunately it hasn't helped either – the door is locked and there are no keys in sight. Perhaps you should try a quieter mode of entry. To try the garage door, turn to 187. To hunt around for a key turn to 407.

341

Your hands are shaking as you press Answer.

'Danny? Is that you?' you ask in a furious whisper. But an unfamiliar voice replies in a flat monotone, making the hair on the back of your neck stand up.

'Don't get involved. You know we're watching you. Back off. Or you're next.'

'Who is this?' you demand; but it seems whoever is calling from Danny's phone doesn't want to chat. You try calling back, but feel suddenly alone and powerless as a mechanical voice tells you 'the mobile you are calling may be switched off'.

You resume your journey in uneasy silence. Turn to 73.

342

You walk to the end of the corridor and put your ear to the door of the kit room. You can hear heavy breathing and shuffling from inside.

You gingerly turn the handle and creep into the room. You are faced with a weasel-faced man called Viv Sprike. He has given you the creeps ever since he was hired as the club's kit man last year, and now you find him with his ear pressed to the wall of your office. He hasn't noticed you come in. You're the boss; how are you going to handle an eavesdropper? Do you:

Fire him on the spot? (Turn to 120)

Ask for his side of the story? (Turn to 145)

Order him to tell you everything and turn out his pockets?

(Turn to 79)

343

As usual, subtract **1** Morale for losing a match. Managing is a thankless job sometimes. Disappointed? You should be. Pick yourself up, and hope that a bunch of no-score draws are coming in at 411.

344

Saturday 12th

You wake early on Saturday morning feeling confident in the ability of your team to go out in front of the home fans and get a result today. Today's needle match is against your local rivals Bridgford City, and the visitors' stand is sure to be packed as this is always one of the more raucous games of the season. For years the home team has always won this fixture. Will you manage to follow tradition? Here are the opposition stats:

> **Bridgford City FC**
> **Overall Skill: 65**
> Dave Curtis is a no-nonsense type of manager, and Bridgford aren't a team for fancy tactics. But their showing so far has been average at best, and defensively they have appeared frail. An opposition with a strong attacking presence should be able to capitalise on this.

Before the match starts, are you in possession of a bleeper? If so, turn to 308. If not, turn to 11.

345
You jam the blade under the sheet of metal and lever it upwards. Underneath is a small, leather-bound diary. You take the book, close the locker door and quickly leave the room. If you wish you may run back to your office to read the diary: turn to 115 before going back to the room plan.

346
Your goalie does the right thing, but unfortunately so does the Bridgford attacker. With a neat sidestep, your goalkeeper is left stranded and it's an open goal. The ball rolls over the line and you're left with that sinking feeling. Note the goal on your Match Sheet, then turn to 80.

347
Monday 31st
Back in your office on Monday morning you go through the post.

Four items in particular catch your eye, and you may examine any or all of them.

A letter marked URGENT (Turn to 3)

A letter stamped with the Football Association logo

(Turn to 394)

A brown parcel (Turn to 316)

The *Hardwick Herald* (Turn to 172)

If you prefer not to waste your precious training time on pushing paperwork, go to 89 to talk to your team about the forthcoming fixtures.

348

If you rolled 6 or more, turn to 150. If you rolled less than 6, turn to 94.

349

Eeurgh. Eleven sweaty, muddy, damp sets of socks and shirts. You start sifting through the pile, when a voice from behind startles you. You spin round.

'Er – sorry, chief. I heard a noise. You OK?'

It's Ben Parker, one of your strikers.

'Thanks, Ben, I'm fine – just, well, nothing really.'

'Sure – well, goodnight, boss.'

A bit embarrassing. But you do find a red boot in the pile, which shouldn't be there. Take it if you like, and go back to the room plan on 107.

350

Saturday 22nd

It's the day of your first away match of the season. Your players are in raucous mood as they board the team bus – they always enjoy travelling. You climb aboard last and greet your regular driver, Eric.

'Don't s'pose you've got the map have you, guv? It wasn't in the usual place.'

The missing route map – you'd forgotten all about it! Do you have it? If so, turn to 72. If not, turn to 174.

351

You may select **two** skills from the list below to dedicate training to this week. Think about where your weaknesses are: is the key to Hardwick's success getting more goals in or keeping more out? Choose which skill you would you like to concentrate on first:

Free kicks (Turn to 87)

Corners (Turn to 470)

Penalties (Turn to 321)

The offside trap (Turn to 233)

Shot-stopping (Turn to 382)

352

The other players have begun to arrive now and you begin the week's training working on passing accuracy. Later in the week you arrange a practice match to observe the players' performance. Do you have Masashi Suda in your squad? If so, turn to 294. If not, turn to 275.

353

Where on earth did you get that? It doesn't fit, I'm afraid. Get back behind your desk where you belong by turning to 281.

354

Roll one dice. If you roll 1–4, turn to 99. If you roll 5 or 6, turn to 268.

355

Your players trudge dejectedly off the pitch while the cheers from the Lowdham Athletic fans echo around the ground. You'll have to do better than that if you want to win the league! Subtract **1** from your team's Morale, and turn to 402 for the rest of the results.

356

Time to select your team! Remember that any players sent off in the last match are not allowed to play today. And if you have any injured players you must roll to see if they have made a full recovery (turn to page 9 for a reminder). When you are ready, turn to 420.

357

Jamie is no stranger to penalties, and carefully watches the eyes of the Papplewick spot-kicker as he takes his run up. It's a dead giveaway, and Coates knows the striker's intentions before the ball even moves. Jamie dives left, and the ball spins towards him. Roll one dice. If you roll 5 or 6, turn to 231. Otherwise turn to 447.

358

Monday 28th

Five days remain before your final away match of the season. It could really improve your chances if you could take at least a point away from this game. You decide to work your squad hard, concentrating on winning balls and keeping possession. But during Wednesday's training session, two players go up for the same high ball and clash heads, sending them sprawling on the ground. Roll two dice.

If you roll 2–5, turn to 363.

If you roll 6 or 7, turn to 142.

If you roll 8 or 9, turn to 98.

If you roll 10–12, turn to 361.

359

Written on the notepaper in Victor's sloping hand is the following:

That's all. Copy down the information if you wish, and place the paper back where you found it. Now what? Have you looked in the glove box yet? To do so turn to 82. To return to your office armed with this new clue, turn to 281.

360

You're in luck. The bathroom window opens on to the car park, and it's wide enough for you to squeeze through. You are able to scramble down a thick growth of ivy on the outside wall, and jump to safety at the bottom. Better get away from here before you have a heart attack. Turn to 384.

361

The two players concerned are Salvatore Duce and Jamie Coates. Both players are now injured, and you must roll in the normal way to see if they can recover in time for the next match (see page 9). Bad luck. Hopefully you've kept back enough players to fill their boots. Turn to 412.

362

For the next match only, add **2** to the Skill of any two of your Defenders. Turn to 6.

363

The two players concerned are Rob Rose and Steve Fitzgerald. Both players are now injured, and you must roll in the normal way to see if they can recover in time for the next match (see page 9). Bad luck. Hopefully you've kept back enough players to fill their boots. Turn to 412.

364

'They will now be looking to turn us over, and you would expect that at this level,' you tell your team. 'But I've seen teams come back from worse positions than this, and I know you've got what it takes to turn this match around.'

'And if we fail?' asks Jamie Coates.

'Then we fail,' you tell him. 'But screw your courage to the goal-post and we'll not fail! Now go out there and get a result.'

Nice one! They look convinced again. Add **2** to your Morale. Remember this will improve your Match Factor as well! When you're ready, you may turn to 448.

365

'Is this it?' you ask, holding out the boot you found in the laundry.

'Meo Deus! You find. Ees good, now I play.'

Problem solved! Add **2** to Carlos de Carvalho's Skill for the next match only, then turn to 215.

366

What a goal! That was worth the season-ticket price alone. The three men at the source of the attack run to the visitors' stand to celebrate in front of two thousand admirers. Has that clinched the match for you? Or was it too little too late? Either way, there's some time left on the clock. Play out the remainder of the match as normal, and when it's finished turn to 397.

367

You step into the players' locker room. It is empty now as your squad has gone home for the day. You may search the place if you like by turning to 90, or alternatively go back to consult your room plan on 107.

368

Turn to 165.

369

Some good business-talk from you ensures that Topflight will be the new name on the Hardwick shirts. Make a note of your new sponsors on your Fact Sheet, then turn to 175.

370

You remember the note, and pat the hard outline of the key in your shirt pocket. Do you wish to use it? If so, turn to 217. If not, turn to 398.

371

You climb the stairs to the executive floor, knock on the heavy oak door marked Chairman and enter the plush office. Victor's leather-topped desk is at one end, and a fat cigar with a wet, chewed end is burning in the ashtray. He can't be far away. Do you have any reason to take a look around? Perform a quick search by turning to 422 if you wish. Otherwise you can sit and breathe the fumes until he returns (turn to 374).

372

You open the door into a pitch-black room. It takes a few seconds to find the light switch, but when you do you realise you're in the storage room. Boxes of merchandise and paperwork line the walls. In the middle is an upturned chest with some playing cards on top, and a small pile of coins. Gambling at work! That's strictly against the rules. Confiscate the evidence if you choose, and return to the room plan on 107.

373

You pick up the receiver. 'Hello?'

The voice on the other end is a whisper, but there's no mistaking it. It's Danny!

His voice is breathless. 'Managed to get away – have to come and get me!'

'Danny! Quick – tell me where you are.'

'In the phone box on the corner of North Street and River View.'

'What's happened to you?'

'He thinks if he can get to me he can win the league. I'll explain when I see you, but come quickly. I'm scared – they said they'd kill me if the police found out!'

'Don't move. I'm on my way.'

But before you can hang up you hear a screech of tyres, a shout, and a sickening thud – then a click as the receiver at the other end is carefully replaced.

Turn to 451.

374

Victor opens the door and waddles in. He is a large man in his mid-fifties, and his bald head glistens with sweat beads from climbing the stairs.

'I hope you don't mind, I let myself in,' you begin, cautiously. 'What did you want to see me about?'

'Oh, just checking up, you know, looking after the troops,' he says uncertainly. 'Terrible thing about Danny, dreadful. Heard anything?' He fixes you with a stare.

The air is sickly yellow with cigar smoke.

'Nothing,' you lie. 'You?'

'No, no, just letting the police do their job. Let them do theirs and we'll do ours. Best way, agreed?'

This is weird and you want to leave. 'Sure,' you say.

'Good, fine, thank you. Goodnight,' he says, and you let yourself out.

Turn to 399.

375

'Absolutely,' you tell him. 'I've got a three-pronged attack in mind for the coming match, and you're the musketeer I want spearheading the outfit. You'll get your ninety. But I need one hundred and ten percent back from you all week.'

Ian beams. 'You won't regret it, chief.'

You may add **1** to Ian Leslie's Skill for the next match. But remember, you've made a promise – and you must play Ian for the full ninety minutes (unless he is injured or sent off). Turn to 352.

376

Play this match in the usual way. Immediately after half-time, turn to 229.

377

Here are the rest of the day's scores for you to study. Complete a new League Table and see where you stand.

```
    Bridgford City 4 — 2 Lowdham Athletic
  Epperstone Town 2 — 2 Lambley Rovers
    Gunthorpe Utd 0 — 1 Woodborough County
 Papplewick Town 0 — 2 Oxton Wanderers
```

If you won or lost your match, make the usual adjustment to your Morale. Ready? Turn to 446.

378

On your way back to Hardwick, Danny explains how he was driven off the road on his way back from the match and pulled from his car. Jack Tatchell and Victor Sinkowski had been waiting for him at the warehouse, and told him he should have joined Oxton Wanderers when he had the chance.

'They said they would decide what to do with me after Oxton won the league and they got rich, but I knew I'd had it really,' he explains.

'You weren't easy to find,' you tell him. 'But I've got proof of the whole thing. We'll get you back to the club now and call the police.'

'Can I use your mobile first? I want to tell Jo I'm coming home.'
Turn to 168.

379

It appears to you in slow motion, but the ball flies irrepressibly past your stranded keeper and into the back of the net. The visitors' stand erupts as you forlornly unwrap a fresh stick of gum. Small comfort. Now turn to 213.

380

The ball seems to be on a collision course with the back of the net. But with lightning reflexes, your Portuguese full-back offers up his knee and the ball ricochets off into no-man's-land to be safely hugged by your goalie. That's what you pay him for! Your supporters in the visitors' stand are on their feet and giving Carlos a standing ovation, which he acknowledges with a toss of his head. If there was anything that rhymed with de Carvalho they'd be singing it now. Get on with the rest of the game and turn to 319 when the curtain comes down.

381

For this match only you may add **1** to the Skill of each of your Midfielders. Now turn to 237 to play your first match!

382

Choose one of your goalkeepers. Now roll one dice. If you roll 1–4, turn to 92. If you roll 5 or 6, turn to 127.

383

Disappointing? You won – how do you think that's going to make your players feel when they read the papers? Lose **2** Morale points. Now turn to 104.

384

There is such a commotion outside the front of the hotel that you are able to leave unnoticed. Jump in your car and head back to the safety of Hardwick City FC by turning to 194.

385

Jonny and Ricky just don't get on. You don't know why, but that's their problem. And yours unfortunately, because from now on you must deduct **2** Skill from each of them while they're both in your squad. Since you've ignored the problem you're going to have to live with it. Subtract **1** Morale due to the sour atmosphere and turn to 60.

386

Roll one dice. If you roll a 1 or 2, turn to 146. If you roll between 3 and 6, turn to 364.

387

'Torrence!' you say, teasing him. 'I see your lads have taken up boxing.'

'This isn't funny,' Jules Torrence begins in a shaky voice. 'Whatever you read in the paper – it's a lie. Yes they were out, but they weren't drunk and they weren't fighting. I've spoken to them. All three swear they were jumped by four men with bats and chains after they'd left the club. This was a professional beating, they're out for the season. I thought of Danny straightaway when I heard. Do you think it's the same crooks?'

Your thoughts are racing. It certainly seems too much to be a coincidence.

'Maybe,' you say. 'Thanks for the call, Jules. See you at the weekend.'

If you had any reason to suspect him before, it now looks like he's as innocent as you are in all of this. Eliminate him from your enquiries and turn to 36.

388

The car lurches as it speeds over the roundabout. Turn to 105.

389

You are being hopelessly outgunned in the centre of the pitch and your players are finding it very hard to play a flowing game. Subtract **5** from your Match Factor for the rest of the match. Now turn to 45.

390

The champagne has been laced with tranquilisers! Roll two dice for each player in your squad. A 2, 3 or 4 means that player has taken one swig too many and might be out of action for the next game. Treat each affected player as though they have an Injury.

If they do not recover properly before the next match they cannot play.

First Danny, now someone is trying to take out your entire squad. Lose **2** Morale after this shocking incident. You resolve to try to get to the bottom of this without further delay. Turn to 48.

391

You tell your players to get on with their own training, while you hunker down to some serious research behind your desk. You spend the week scouring the newspapers for clues, you even phone a couple of journalist friends for inside knowledge, but you draw a blank. At least you tried. Turn to 419.

392

You decide to spend the rest of your weekend at home. Unfortunately, there was information hidden in Victor's house that you need; without it, Danny will never make it out alive and his body will be found floating in the river a month from now. Maybe you made a bad decision somewhere along the way; or maybe you weren't bold enough. Either way, your adventure is over this time. Turn to 101.

393

Turn to 154.

394

The letter is official-looking and addressed to you. You rip it open and begin to read.

To: The Manager, Hardwick City FC

Notification of Transfer Window

The following players are available for immediate transfer. All offers must be received by the end of the week, according to FA regulations.

This is an opportunity to build up your squad! Two names stand out in particular:

Jonny Steel

Position: Defender (Skill 7)

Born: Newcastle 11/3/86

Height: 5ft 10in

Weight: 11st 2lb

Last Season's Stats:

Goals: 1

Yellow Cards: 3

Red Cards: 0

Considered one of the up-and-coming full-backs at this level of football, and widely tipped to win his first cap this year for the England U-21s. Serious, strong and solid.

Masashi Suda

Position: Attacker (Skill 6)

Born: Osaka 9/12/84

Height: 5ft 8in

Weight: 10st 6lb

Last Season's Stats:

Goals: 7

Yellow Cards: 1

Red Cards: 1

Since Japan's impressive showing in the 2002 World Cup, the floodgates have opened for signings of young Japanese soccer players. An ambitious young centre-forward, Masashi is no exception to the Japanese reputation of playing tireless, high-speed football.

This is also your opportunity to make some sales. Interest has been expressed in two of your current squad: Michael Hurley and Joe Fry.

The market is open! You can buy and sell any combination of these players. What do you want to do first?

Put in a bid for Jonny Steel? (Turn to 324)
Put in a bid for Masashi Suda? (Turn to 296)
See what you can get for Joe Fry? (Turn to 86)
See what you can get for Michael Hurley? (Turn to 52)

You're under no obligations here. If you're perfectly happy with your squad the way it is, turn to 228.

395

2:45pm

You lead your team down the tunnel in the direction of the noisy fans. Rumours were that this game would be a sell-out and the most highly televised match all year. Your players are keyed up and eager for the match to start. As they file out on to the pitch, Danny stops briefly to talk to you.

'Thanks for this chance, chief. Hope I can remember the rules.'

You laugh. 'Hey – you forgot this,' and you hand him the captain's armband. Danny pulls it up on to his sleeve, and shakes your hand. 'Now go out there and have a good time,' you tell him.

It takes a few moments for the crowd to believe their eyes, but all of a sudden the noise level rises ten times. Everyone, including the away fans and the Epperstone players, is on their feet and giving Danny a rapturous standing ovation. You watch from the mouth of the tunnel for a few minutes, then make your way to the dugout. When the fans see you the noise goes right up again

– yes, they're clapping you – and you wave to all sides of the ground in acknowledgment.

The excitement is so high that the referee has to delay kick-off by ten minutes, but eventually the game is under way. The mood is good, almost like a friendly, and the referee keeps cautions to a minimum. A neat, straight pass from Klaus Wehnert in the thirty-eighth minute sees Ben Parker clear on goal, and he slots a low ball past the Epperstone keeper. One-nil.

At half-time you ask Danny how he's doing, but he's keen to stay on the field so you let him. The second half begins at a furious tempo and there are a number of chances squandered at either end, but after ten minutes the pace slackens off as it always does. And then, in the seventy-seventh minute, the sequence of events that will stay in your mind for ever. Frost has the ball in space on the left. He looks up and lofts a high ball to John Hoggart in the centre circle. A one-two with Duce to his right, then a beautiful through-ball to Knox leaving one defender stranded. Danny picks up the pace twenty-five yards out, jumping to avoid a sliding tackle from the Epperstone sweeper. He makes up more ground – twenty yards, eighteen – and all the while Parker is to his left, matching him stride for stride. An Epperstone full-back commits himself to a charge, and Danny Knox slots the ball to Parker who takes it on the run. Danny has to swerve to avoid the late tackle but rights himself and crosses the line into the box. Ben is being closed down quickly by the remaining defence, and an expectant hush descends over the crowd. He manages to hold his course until the last second, then toe-pokes the ball into Danny's path before being bundled over. The angle is tight – too tight, surely – and the goalie is closing the gap well. But Danny's vision is excellent and his timing perfect, as he chips the ball just out of reach of the committed keeper. And, just as he intended, it dips underneath the crossbar and over the white line.

You're on your feet and cheering, but you can't even hear yourself beneath the exultant thunderclap that booms from the fans on all sides of the ground. Danny is mobbed by the players, and you're unable to suppress a laugh of joy as you look back to

where Viv has joined you in the dugout as your guest of honour. Viv gives you the thumbs-up, and winks.

Turn to 472.

396

Play out the remainder of the game in the normal way. When the ref's whistle blows for full-time, turn to 76.

397

Here are the rest of the day's match results.

```
   Bridgford City 0 — 0 Lambley Rovers
  Epperstone Town 1 — 2 Oxton Wanderers
  Gonalston City 1 — 0 Woodborough County
 Papplewick Town 5 — 3 Lowdham Athletic
```

You know the routine. Complete a fresh League Table, and see where Hardwick City FC stands. Then turn to 297.

398

You return to your office before locking up and heading home for the rest of the weekend. Turn to 208.

399

Monday 17th

You've got an away match coming up in a few days against Oxton Wanderers. You must decide how best to spend your time. If you work in your office, going over your notes and phoning around to see what else you can discover, turn to 391. If you think you ought to spend some time with your players to prepare them for Saturday's match, turn to 132.

400

Here's what you're up against this week.

Papplewick Town FC
Overall Skill: 60

Sam Shaughnessy's tactic is to overload the midfield to stifle the opposition. Papplewick are not the strongest team, however, and a recognised counter-measure is to fight fire with fire. Sam says he knows what he's doing.

Half an hour until kick-off, and you're back where you belong. A pity Danny Knox isn't – nothing would thrill your fans more than if he were to lead your team to glory this afternoon. But nothing new has come to light all week. 'This one's for him,' you think to yourself.

'All right, lads,' you begin, and they all stop chattering and turn their eyes to you. 'I want you to go out there and give it everything you've got. I want to see passion and commitment. Keep your heads above water and your feet on the ground. And whatever they dish up for you, serve it right back to them.'

'Anything else, boss?' asks Jamie Coates with a wry grin as your players trot down the tunnel.

'Just keep it real, Jimbo,' you tell him, giving his bald head a friendly rub.

Select your team for this match and work out your Match

Factor. Now go out there and take what's yours. When the ref's watch says 30 minutes, turn to 65.

401

Trying to look for all the world like you own the car, but feeling like a petty thief, you climb inside. The leather upholstery is polished to a shine, and the walnut dashboard reeks of wealth. On the passenger seat is a jacket which you can search by turning to 290. If you'd prefer to search the glove compartment, turn to 82.

402

Here are the results from the day's other games.

```
        Bridgford City 1 — 1 Epperstone Town
         Gunthorpe Utd 3 — 2 Gonalston City
        Lambley Rovers 0 — 2 Oxton Wanderers
    Woodborough County 4 — 0 Papplewick Town
```

Fill in the League Table on your Fact Sheet. Remember, a win scores 3 points for that team, a draw scores 1, and a loss scores zero. Put the team with the highest number of points at the top and the lowest at the bottom. If two teams have the same number of points, arrange them in order of Goal Difference. Remember to include Lowdham and Hardwick in the table! When you have finished doing this, turn to 408.

403

You lock the door behind you as the answering machine clicks into life. But you stop dead as you hear a familiar voice on the other end. It's Danny!

'Hello? Damn . . . If you're there pick up!!'

You fumble with the keys in the lock as Danny's breathless voice continues.

'I got away – look, I'm in the phonebox on the corner of North Street and River View. He thinks if he can get to me he can win the league. They said they'll kill me if the police find out . . . I'm scared . . . if you can hear this, just come and get me!'

Lunging over the desk you grab the handset.

'Danny! It's me – don't move, I'm on my way.'

But before he can reply you hear the sound of screeching tyres, men's voices, and a sickening thud – then a click as the receiver at the other end is carefully replaced.

Do you replay the message (turn to 167)? Or hurry to the phonebox (turn to 451)?

404

Your chosen players have responded exceptionally well in training. For the rest of the season, whenever the opposing team scores a goal, roll two dice. If you roll 10, 11 or 12, treat the shot as offside. Make a note of this on your Fact Sheet next to this Defender's name (it only applies if he is playing). Remember: you can focus on two skills this week. If this was your first, turn back to 351 to choose again from the list. If you have now chosen two, turn to 430.

405

Lowdham Athletic have taken three wins from three games.

Certainly an impressive record, and quite a bit better than yours. The award is duly presented to manager Bill Drebble. You send him a fax by way of congratulations, but secretly you feel a bit envious. You'll have to make some improvements in the remainder of your games if you're going to catch them. Now turn to 347.

406

'So is one of you going to tell me what the problem is then?' you ask with a resigned smile.

'Like I said, he wants my regular spot,' Ricky moans.

'That's crap, chief,' protests Jonny. 'I'm just trying to get on with it, but he's playing like I'm not there.'

'OK, lads. You've both got your regular positions due to merit,' you tell them firmly. 'To keep your places in the team you'll need to work together, any less and you bring the team down with you. You know I don't have favourites, but you also know I won't stand for unprofessionalism.'

They shuffle their feet but don't have much to complain about. You can't work miracles, and if two people can't get on there's not much you can do about it. But you've defused a tricky situation, and the two agree to play the remainder of the match amicably. However, if you play them together at the back again, you must subtract **1** from each of their Skills because of their inability to cooperate properly.

Now turn to 60.

407

Where do you look first? Under the mat (turn to 309)? Or under the flowerpots (turn to 62)?

408

Since Danny's disappearance, every sports reporter and their dog has been wanting to interview you. It would be a full-time job talking to them all, so a press conference has been arranged for after today's match in one of the club's many meeting rooms. You could do without this . . . But maybe it will shut them up and stop the back-page speculation for a while. You push open the door and enter. Turn to 218.

409

Will Frost seems to have reached a peak of physical fitness this week. He is chasing down every loose ball in the midfield, and using speed and agility to create space for himself. A Woodborough centre-half is storming down the left flank but Frost takes him on and wins the ball in a well-timed challenge. The winger goes over, but the referee waves play on and Frost surges forward to the eighteen-yard line. Before the defenders have time to react, he chips a beauty into the box to pick out Ben

Parker. Ben takes it on his chest, lets it bounce once, and takes a kick from a perfect position. Roll two dice for this expert manoeuvre. If you roll less than 9, turn to 413. If you roll 9 or more, turn to 41.

410

It's going to be close this month! Both you and Lowdham Athletic manager Bill Drebble are unbeaten so far, with an impressive record of two wins and a draw. Get your Goal Difference from your latest League Table. Now subtract the total number of red and yellow cards your players have been shown in your three matches to date. Is your number:

Less than 3?   (Turn to 100)
3 or more?   (Turn to 32)

411

Here are the results from the rest of the day's play.

```
    Gonalston City 3 — 1 Bridgford City
   Epperstone Town 0 — 0 Gunthorpe Utd
 Lowdham Athletic 2 — 0 Woodborough County
  Papplewick Town 2 — 2 Lambley Rovers
```

Fill in the second League Table and see where you stand. (You might find it easier to make the changes on the table you filled in last time, then copy the new details across.) When you have finished, turn to 253.

412

The rest of the training week goes uneventfully and the atmosphere in the team is good despite the injuries. Turn to 440.

413

You've heard strikers talk before about the sweet spot of their boot, and you reckon Ben has hit it this time. The ball is struck with precision and timing, and it seems to have a homing device as it first rises high and wide of the goalie's outstretched glove then dips perfectly to find the inside netting. The stands are packed with your home supporters and they howl their delight as the ball drops over the line. Gladiatorial Rome was never like this! Leap up and punch the air, or sit and smile quietly to yourself – it's up to you. Then turn to 396.

414

```
    Bridgford City 0 — 2 Gunthorpe Utd
   Gonalston City 3 — 0 Epperstone Town
 Oxton Wanderers 0 — 1 Lowdham Athletic
  Lambley Rovers 1 — 2 Woodborough County
```

Update the League Table and see where you stand. (Remember to change your Morale if you won or lost.) When you are ready, turn to 74.

415

Your chosen player has responded well in training, and his corners have become longer and more accurate. For the rest of the season, you may add **1** to the dice roll whenever this player takes a corner (make a note of this on your Fact Sheet). Remember: you can focus on two skills this week. If this was your first, turn back to 351 to choose again from the list. If you have now chosen two, turn to 430.

416

Congratulations! Your first match in charge this season, and three points scored. Your players are in high spirits despite the events of the past week: add **1** to your team's Morale. Now turn to 402 to see how the other teams in the league fared.

417

Danny Knox might have been at the start of this terror campaign, but he certainly wasn't their only target. Poor José – you know exactly how he feels. If you ever had reason to suspect him in Danny's abduction before, you can be pretty sure now he isn't involved. Make a note of these new findings on your Fact Sheet. Lock up securely for the night and turn to 232.

418

Did you lose or draw today? If so, turn to 104. If you won, turn to 383.

419

You've got an important fixture coming up. Have you spent *any* time with your players this week, or have you been running around thinking you're Sherlock Holmes the whole time? Be honest. If you've dedicated some time to training your squad, turn to 350. If not, turn to 287.

420

> **Oxton Wanderers FC**
> **Overall Skill: 63**
> Oxton have a reputation – some say an unfair one – for playing boring football. Their strikers are certainly less than flamboyant and their defence is rock-solid. Manager Jack Tatchell seems to consider winning less important than not losing.

Enter your players on your next Match Sheet. Then work out your Match Factor just like before. Can you lead your team to an important victory against the 'One-all Wanderers'? Turn to 181.

421

Saturday 29th

You never get tired of that special buzz when you wake up on a Saturday morning, knowing that today you're leading your team into a crucial head-to-head with quality opposition! Wonderful. A small knot of home supporters is already queuing outside the gates as you arrive, and they cheer as you sweep past security and into the ground. When you're ready, turn to 400 to go and meet the players in the dressing room.

422

The first place you look is his desk drawer, and in there is the very thing you have been missing: your driver's route map. And someone's added a strange diagram to one of the top corners:

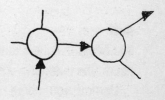

Why did Victor just take it from your office without asking? If you dare, you may take it right back again (make a note of it on your Fact Sheet). But better pretend you've only just arrived, because the door is opening. Turn to 374.

423

As the players climb aboard the team bus, you notice that Will Frost and Ian Leslie are deeply engaged in a discussion. They are last to board, and their whispering continues as the bus moves away. Will you ask them what's going on (turn to 51) or leave them to it (turn to 91)?

424

You remain in the background, sitting with your physios and coaching staff in the dugout. You get a perfect view from here, and you are able to keep a close eye on your players' performances. Play the match in the normal way, and when half-time comes turn to 224.

425

You notice that Jonny Steel and Ricky Neville are sitting away from the pack and each other, with venomous looks on their faces. You're the boss: what's best? Should you take them to one side for a talk (turn to 5), or leave it (turn to 385)?

426

You begin making excuses but there is a click and the line goes dead. She'll be long gone before you can get to her.

'Damn!' you shout, slamming down the phone. You head

home for the weekend, confused and disappointed. Turn to 280.

427

Jed is pleased to be singled out for praise. The same cannot be said for the remainder of the forwards, who are demoralised by your words.

'What's he got that we haven't? I knew you had favourites in this team,' Ian Leslie says bitterly.

Oh dear. For the next match only, add **1** to Jed's Skill but subtract **1** from the Skill of whichever Attackers play alongside him. Better keep player talks where they belong – in private. Now turn to 34.

428

'Yes?'

'Who is this?' you ask.

The voice replies with a question. 'Is that *Newsdesk*?'

You realise you must be speaking to a reporter. What do you tell her? If you claim to be a newspaper editor, turn to 246. If you decide it's best to stick to the truth, turn to 257.

429

You're up there at the top, and you have to make sure you stay there. No reason why you can't do just that; you've obviously got the measure of this management game. But don't get complacent. A couple of poor performances and the table could collapse under you like a house of cards. And sorry to rain on your parade, but there's that small matter of rescuing your erstwhile top striker, Danny Knox. Ready? Then turn to 437.

430

Make a note of your team's new strengths on your Fact Sheet. Remember, certain skills may only apply to a specific player; and if this player is out because of an injury or a match ban, you do not benefit from this particular bonus until he returns. Now turn to 344.

431

Did you sell your striker Toby Wood to Lambley a couple of weeks ago? If so, turn to 264. If you still have him in your squad, turn to 50.

432

Once again you thank your squad for their performances, and once again you find yourself in your office on a Saturday evening. During your adventure so far, perhaps you have eavesdropped on a telephone conversation. If so, you'll have heard about a meeting which took place recently – now might be a good time to go to the scene of that meeting in search of more clues as to Danny's whereabouts. Where would you like to visit?

Gonalston   (Turn to 176)
Gunthorpe   (Turn to 200)
Oxton   (Turn to 393)
Woodborough (Turn to 20)

Alternatively you can call it a day and retire for the weekend by turning to 358.

433

'I suggest you speak with your lawyer,' you are told at the police station. 'You do understand how serious this is?'

How will they ever believe you? You know you've been framed. And even if you suspect who is behind all this, you are being suspended from your job – 'pending a full investigation'. Your adventure is over, and you should now turn to 101.

434

Oh, come off it, ref! He dived! You and your fans are unanimous on the subject, but the referee has fallen for it and raises his arm to award the free kick. It's in a dangerous spot, just outside the penalty area. Roll for a free kick in the usual way, where a 5 or 6 means a goal to Bridgford. When the drama is over, turn to 80.

435

You jiggle it and coax it and eventually your frustration snaps it in the lock. You're left with a small piece of metal and a red face. Go back to your office and get on with your day job by turning to 398.

436

'It's Pete, boss. Something's happened you ought to know about.'

Pete Stoneman is your best talent scout, and is responsible for having found many of your youth players in the first place. He continues in a guarded voice.

'I've been down the Woodborough ground to have a look at José Torrego's men, see if there's anyone we could use if they came on the market. Thing is, there's no one there – not training anyway. Place is swarming with cop cars – bomb squad mainly, there was a tip-off this morning. Apparently some of the players got letters telling them to stay away today and not play tomorrow either. There are loads of rumours going around but one of the hacks was pretty sure Torrego's been threatened too. He's going to find it hard to get a team together for their match tomorrow.'

A chill that started at the bottom of your spine has spread to your neck.

'Thanks, Pete. See you tomorrow.'

Turn to 417.

437

On the journey home the team bus gets stuck in traffic. You've finished going through the notes you made on your player performances, and the players are dozing and chatting quietly to each other behind you. You stare out of the window at the large houses, and realise you've been here once before – when you were offered the job, Victor had invited you round to his house for dinner. Wasn't that round here somewhere? If you have a good reason to go there again, turn to 184. If not, turn to 392.

438

Your strong midfield presence is more than equal to the job, and your players are passing the ball around with confidence. Add **2** to your Match Factor for the rest of this game. Now turn to 45.

439

During training this week you are particularly impressed by the solidity of your back three. They are collecting dangerous balls with ease and seem to have perfected the offside trap. Add **1** to the Skill of any <u>two</u> of your Defenders for this match only. Now turn to 421.

440

Saturday 3rd

Fortunately your last away game of the season is at Lambley – not too far away, and something of a local derby so you can be sure your supporters will turn out in their numbers to make a big noise. You greet your squad as they board the team bus, and you take some time to study the form of your hosts during the short journey to their home ground.

Lambley Rovers FC
Overall Skill: 62

Lambley play a very attacking game, and they're generally reckoned to be one of the most exciting teams to watch. Eric Redman's men have had a run of bad form lately, and stand no chance of winning the league. But don't be fooled: with a couple of new signings up front, your defence had better be ready.

Select your team carefully for this vital fixture. When you have done so, turn to 431.

441

You dash to your car and jump inside, just as Victor's dark green Jaguar growls past the security gate and sweeps up the road to the left. Turn to 114.

442

Uh-oh. A long ball from the Lambley defence has found the feet of their attacking midfielder, and he's beaten the offside trap. He's off and running in the penalty area with only your keeper in his way, and his foot connects powerfully with the ball.

Roll one dice and add the number to your keeper's Skill. Now roll two dice for the shot. If this roll is higher, turn to 71. Otherwise turn to 258.

443

Saturday 24th

You and Danny Knox drive to work together in the morning. You arrive late on purpose, so that the whole squad is already assembled in the dressing room.

You open the door and greet them. 'Bit of a change of plan today, boys,' you tell them. 'Ben, Jed, you're up front today.'

'Just two – but we always play three forwards,' protests Ben Parker.

'That's what we practise, bossman,' complains Salvatore Duce.

'That's what we're doing,' says Danny, poking his head past you. 'Morning, lads.'

There is uproar in the dressing room as the players clamber over each other to greet their colleague, a bit like if Father Christmas walked into a classroom of five-year-olds. You give them a few minutes to finish slapping his back and for the questions to die down, before clapping your hands together loudly.

'I see you all remember Mr Knox, then,' you say. 'We've got a game to play today, no different from any other. Get changed, back here for two.'

Viv Sprike is waiting for you as you leave the room, and your eyes brighten when you see him.

'Viv! What can I do for you?'

'Well, there is one thing,' he says with a smirk.

Turn to 395.

444

It's written into the terms of your management contract that the club's funds must always stay in the black. You have broken that agreement, and the accountants will be presenting their findings to the board. It's too late for you: already your boss Victor Sinkowski has your replacement lined up. Someone with a little more business acumen . . . Turn to 101.

445

As the week goes on you notice a marked improvement in your midfielders, who are playing supportively. But your defenders seem too keen to get rid of the ball and are making some foolish errors. For the next match only, add **2** to the Skill of one of your Midfielders but subtract **1** from the Skill of two of your playing Defenders. Now turn to 34.

446

The atmosphere in the bus on the way back to Hardwick is rowdy as ever, but you're not in the mood this time. It's been weeks now since Danny's disappearance and neither the police nor you seem to be any closer to getting him back safely. You recline your seat, and stare out through rain-spattered windows as the featureless motorway races past. It's hypnotic, and you begin to doze off when you are woken by the sudden vibration of your mobile. You look at the display:

> **Danny Knox**
> **Answer?**

Do you answer it (turn to 341) or not (turn to 73)?

447

Coates is more than equal to the shot, and punches the ball cleanly away! It's picked up by your defence and hoofed into safety. Let your goalie enjoy his hero's ovation, and turn to 213.

448

Make any team substitutions you like (remember you can't have more than three in any one match!). Now get out there and play the second half. When you get to 90 minutes, turn to 64.

449

Your wingers and central midfielders are showing impressive passing ability this week, and are serving up pinpoint crosses for your strikers. Add **1** to the Skill of any <u>two</u> of your Midfielders for this match only. Now turn to 421.

450

You pick up the object. It's a black wallet, and the leather feels warm in your hand. It's not Danny's . . . Inside it is a small amount of cash, some receipts and a torn scrap of paper with some writing on it:

Room 2
THE SH
No. 13

You slip the paper into your pocket. Copy down what it says carefully on your Fact Sheet. Climbing back into your car, you start the engine and set off home. Turn to 274.

451

You bolt from the office, and jump into your car. That call box is only a few minutes away. Maybe if you're quick you'll make it in time . . .

But when you arrive the place is deserted. There's the phonebox, but no sign of a car – or of Danny. You can see tyre marks on the road, and a slick of oil leading away from them and down the road.

Do you follow the trail (turn to 28)? Or would you prefer to search the phonebox (turn to 149)?

452

Two yellows equals a red, and the home fans stand and boo as Steve gets his marching orders. He'll be out for the next game now. Turn to 169.

453

What will you do? If you leave the way you came, turn to 30. To take your chances out of the bathroom window, turn to 360.

454

You may continue buying and selling players if you wish. But remember you may only deal with each player once. If you haven't already, you may:

Put in a bid for Jonny Steel (Turn to 324)
Put in a bid for Masashi Suda (Turn to 296)
See what you can get for Joe Fry (Turn to 86)
See what you can get for Michael Hurley (Turn to 52)

If you've done enough dealing this time, turn to 228.

455

You swing the car left on to Bridge Lane, and put your foot to the floor. Turn to 196.

456

The tail lights of the car in front of you flare red as the driver slows to a stop, and you slam on the brakes. A gaggle of schoolchildren is crossing in front of you, and beyond them you see Victor disappearing into the distance. Sitting there tapping your foot won't help. What will you do? To give up and return to sanity, turn to 281. If you prefer to stay in pursuit turn to 177.

457

Staplers, hole punches, paper clips – what exactly are you looking for? There's a steel letter-opener which you may wish to take.

Pocket whatever else you want, remembering to make a note of it all on your Fact Sheet, and return to the room plan at 107.

458

Klaus is pleased to be singled out for praise. The same cannot be said for the remainder of the midfielders, who are demoralised by your words.

'We're all working hard as well, you know!' complains Will Frost.

Oops. For the next match only, add **1** to Klaus's Skill but subtract **1** from the Skill of whichever Midfielders play alongside him. Better keep player talks where they belong – in private. Now turn to 34.

459

You take the most direct route to The Ship Hotel, and pull up in the car park behind the building half an hour later. You enter through a revolving door and find yourself in a busy lobby full of guests and luggage, so you are able to make your way up the staircase unnoticed. You run up two flights of stairs to the second floor, nearly knocking over two tall men in black suits who seem to be in just as much of a hurry to get down. You find room 209 with ease, and knock sharply. No answer. You try the handle, and the door swings open. But what you see inside makes you wish you'd never made that call. Turn to 8.

460

You swing the car round to the right, narrowly avoiding an HGV whose driver slams on his horn ungraciously. You wobble for a moment, but straighten up and continue along the road. Behind you, the black saloon with the single dim headlight does the same. Judging by the numbered warehouses lining the road either side of you, it appears you're now in some sort of industrial estate. In less than half a mile you reach another crossroads. Deserted streets leave in every direction. Do you drive:

Left on to Chestnut Drive? (Turn to 93)
Straight ahead on to Spindle View? (Turn to 327)
Right on to Tithe Lane? (Turn to 216)

461

You recognise the gun as the one you found in Victor's glove box. The bullets are still in your desk drawer . . .

'Are you sure that gun's loaded?' you ask Victor cautiously.

'How pathetic,' Victor sneers. 'The condemned man tries to buy some time. Goodnight, Mr Knox.'

He squeezes the trigger. Click. Again – another click, strangely loud in the silent room. Victor Sinkowski looks up and his fleshy mouth really does drop open. You and Danny look at one another, and with a double yell you launch yourselves at the fat man with the gun. Victor doesn't stand a chance as your shoulders connect with his bulky frame, and he gives half a yelp before the impact knocks the wind from his lungs. He staggers backwards, and you wince at the sound as the back of his head smacks against the door frame.

Danny raises his fist above Victor's unconscious face, but you grab his wrist tightly. 'Too good for him, Dan. Let the police take over now.' Turn to 269.

462

You can't help feeling a little disappointed as Victor pulls up in a half-empty car park, and you realise he's come out to do nothing more sinister than a little shopping. No doubt he's stocking up on single malt and fine cigars, you grumble to yourself as he shuts the car door, smoothes down his suit and saunters towards the arcade. Ah, life on the Board. But then a thought occurs to you. Do you see if he's left his car door open (turn to 191), or head back to your office (turn to 281)?

463

Who do you have in mind? Maybe you'd like to improve one of your strikers to compensate for the loss of Danny's right-boot magic. Or perhaps you feel your defence is letting you down. Whoever you single out, begin their ball-skills programme by rolling one dice.

If you roll 1, 2, 3 or 4, add **1** to that player's Skill.

If you roll 5 or 6, add **2** to that player's Skill.

When you have finished, turn to 419.

464

The more money you offer for this Croatian midfielder, the more likely you are to get him. But don't overdo it! First, decide how many millions you'd like to offer. Then roll one dice and add this to your bid. If the number is **higher** than Ivan Najev's Skill (7), congratulations: your offer is accepted! Add his name to your Fact Sheet and welcome him to Hardwick City FC (don't forget to deduct the money you spend from your Budget). If it's equal or lower, you've been refused.

You only get one go at this. When proceedings are over, turn to 199.

465

For this match only you may add **1** to the Skill of each of your Defenders. Now turn to 237 to play your first match!

466

You make your way over to Victor's house, a rather fine five-bedroom affair on Elvendon Drive with ivy growing up the sides and a small orchard for a front garden. The place looks deserted, and there's no sign of him or his car. How are you going to get in? Do you:

Smash one of the front door windows? (Turn to 247)
Try the garage door?   (Turn to 187)
Hunt around for a key?   (Turn to 407)

467

In John Hoggart's mind the ball is already in the back of the net, and his intended cross into the path of Toby Wood is less than perfect. Wood has to check his stride, by which time the Gunthorpe back line has had some time to regroup and the ball is bundled out for a corner to you. Take this corner as normal, then play out the remainder of the game in the usual way. When the match is over, turn to 397.

468

As the traffic begins to creep forward, you try to maintain a safe distance. You can still see Victor's car up ahead, and wherever he's going he doesn't seem to be in much of a hurry to get there. You pick up speed to match his, but just as you begin to feel you've got the hang of these covert operations you see another set of lights up ahead just changing to amber. Sinkowski's Jaguar sails through them, and you will the cars between you to keep going . . . Roll one dice. If you roll 1 or 2, turn to 21. If you roll 3–6, turn to 456.

469

Your chosen player has responded well in training. For the rest of the season, you may add **1** to the dice roll whenever this player takes a free kick (make a note of this on your Fact Sheet). Remember: you can focus on two skills this week. If this was your first, turn back to 351 to choose again from the list. If you have now chosen two, turn to 430.

470

Choose a team member to be your regular corner-taker. Now roll one dice. If you roll 1 or 2, turn to 78. If you roll 3–6, turn to 415.

471

After the press conference you walk back to your office, tired from the pressure and the excitement of the football. Antek Bobak and Jed Stevens pass you in the corridor.

'It's been ages since Danny went missing,' Stevens says. 'Is there any news?'

'Not yet. But I'm confident we'll hear something soon.' You feel bad lying to your players, but you don't tell them about the phone call last night. You just can't risk it.

In your office, there is a message waiting for you on your answerphone. You press play, and the braying voice of your club chairman addresses you.

'Victor here. It's Saturday morning. Come and see me after the match, please.'

Turn to 221.

Turn the page for paragraph 472 . . .

```
        Hardwick City 2 — 0 Epperstone Town
 Woodborough County 0 — 1 Bridgford City
     Papplewick Town 2 — 1 Gonalston City
     Lambley Rovers 0 — 0 Lowdham Athletic
    Oxton Wanderers A — A Gunthorpe Utd
```

Gunthorpe United are awarded 1 point due to abandoned match.

Final League Table

Final Position	Team name	Goals For	Goals Against	Goal Difference	Points
1					
2					
3					
4					
5					
6					
7					
8					
9					
10					

You've won the league!

Match Sheet: Saturday 15th

Hardwick City 2 **vs** 1 **Lowdham Athletic**

Team Selection

No.	Position	Player name	Skill	Injuries, cards
2	Goalkeeper	Rob Rose	5	2 Y cards
3	Defender	S. Fitsgerald	5	J Y cards
4	Defender	A. Sobok	5	IY, 1R
5	Def/Mid	M. Hurrly	5	JY, IR
6	Def/Mid	J. Frost	5	1Y
7	Midfielder	K. Welrent	6	1Y
8	Midfielder	J. haggort	4	2Y, 1R
9	Mid/Att	I. leslie	6	1Y
10	Mid/Att	J stevens	6	1Y
11	Attacker	T Wood	8	2Y, 2R
12	Attacker	B. Barker	6	2Y 2R

NB subtract 2 from the Skill of any player playing outside his normal position for this match.

Overall Skill		Opponent Skill		Morale		Fitness		Home Advantage		Match Factor
56	−	66	+	27	+	32	+	3	=	59

If your MF is more than zero, add 1 to your dice rolls. If it is less than zero, you must subtract 1.

Referee's Watch		15	30	45	60	75	90

League Table

Put the teams in order of points.
If two teams have the same number of points, the one with the best Goal Difference comes higher.
If they have the same Goal Difference, put them in order of Goals For.

Position	Team name	Goals For	Goals Against	Goal Difference	Points
1	Woodborough	4	4	4	3
2	Gunthorpe	3	3	3	3
3	Hardwick	2	2	2	3
4	Oxton wanders	2	2	2	3
5	~~Oonles~~	1	1	1	1
6	Powdham	0	0	0	0
7	Bridgeford	1	1	1	1
8	Epperstone	1	1	1	1
9	Lambly Rovers	0	0	0	0
10	Papplewick	0	0	0	0

Win = 3 points
Draw = 1 point
Lose = 0 points

Goal Difference = Goals For − Goals Against

Match Sheet: Saturday 22nd

Oxton Wanderers ☐2 vs ☐3 Hardwick City

Team Selection

No.	Position	Player name	Skill	Injuries, cards
2	Goalkeeper	C. de carvolho	6	1 y 1 R
3	Defender	S. Fitsgerald	5	
4	Defender	R. Neville	4	
5	Def/Mid	Rob.Rose	5	
6	Def/Mid	J.hoggart	4	
7	Midfielder	A. Robok	5	
8	Midfielder	W. Frost	5	
9	Mid/Att	R. Parker	5	
10	Mid/Att	Salvotero	5	
11	Attacker	T. Wood	6	
12	Attacker	K. Wehrent	6	

NB subtract 2 from the Skill of any player playing outside his normal position for this match.

Overall Skill		Opponent Skill		Morale		Fitness		Home Advantage		Match Factor
56	−	53	+	12	+	7	−	3	=	9

If your MF is more than zero, add 1 to your dice rolls. If it is less than zero, you must subtract 1.

Referee's Watch

15	30	45	60	75	90

League Table

Put the teams in order of points.

If two teams have the same number of points, the one with the best Goal Difference comes higher.

If they have the same Goal Difference, put them in order of Goals For.

Position	Team name	Goals For	Goals Against	Goal Difference	Points
1	Hardwick	5	5	5	6
2	Gunthorpe	3	3	3	4
3	Woodborugh	4	4	4	3
4	Oxton won.	4	4	4	3
5	Lambham	2	2	2	3
6	gonst city	3	3	5	4
7	Bridgeford.	2	2	2	1
8	Pamplewick	2	3	2	1
9	lambly	3	2	2	1
10	epperstone	0	0	0	2

Win = 3 points
Draw = 1 point
Lose = 0 points

Goal Difference = Goals For – Goals Against

Match Sheet: Saturday 29th

Hardwick City 4 **vs** 2 **Papplewick Town**

Team Selection

No.	Position	Player name	Skill	Injuries, cards
2	Goalkeeper	R. Reed	5	
3	Defender	S. Fitsgrald	6	
4	Defender	K. Wehrent	6	
5	Def/Mid	J. Krost	5	
6	Def/Mid	J. hoggart	4	
7	Midfielder	So lveter	5	
8	Midfielder	R. Neville	5	
9	Mid/Att	B. Parker	5	
10	Mid/Att	A. Kobpk	5	
11	Attacker	T. wood	6	
12	Attacker	carlohos	8	

NB subtract 2 from the Skill of any player playing outside his normal position for this match.

Overall Skill	Opponent Skill	Morale	Fitness	Home Advantage	Match Factor
60	− 60	+ 15	+ 16	+ 3 =	34

If your MF is more than zero, add 1 to your dice rolls. If it is less than zero, you must subtract 1.

Referee's Watch	15	30	45	60	75	90

League Table

Put the teams in order of points.
If two teams have the same number of points, the one with the best Goal Difference comes higher.
If they have the same Goal Difference, put them in order of Goals For.

Position	Team name	Goals For	Goals Against	Goal Difference	Points
1	Handwick	9	9	9	9
2	Gonol city	6	6	6	7
3	Gunthorpe	5		5 5	7
4	Woodbourgh	6	6	6	6
5	Lowdham	3	3	3	6
6	Oxtom won.	3.	3	3	3
7	Bridgeford	1	1	1	4
8	Epperstone	2	2	2	2
9	Lambly	2	2	1	1
10	Piplewick	2	2	2	1

Win = 3 points
Draw = 1 point
Lose = 0 points

Goal Difference = Goals For – Goals Against

Match Sheet: Saturday 5th

Gonalston City ☐ **vs** ☐ **Hardwick City**

Team Selection

No.	Position	Player name	Skill	Injuries, cards
2	Goalkeeper	R. REED	5	
3	Defender	J. Fitsgerald	6	
4	Defender	K. Wehrohet	6	
5	Def/Mid	W. Frost	5	
6	Def/Mid	A. Bobok	5	
7	Midfielder	Solveterd	5	
8	Midfielder	J. Olbggort	6	
9	Mid/Att	Ren. P.	6	
10	Mid/Att	R. Neville	7	
11	Attacker	St. Wood	6	
12	Attacker	Garlahos	6	

NB subtract 2 from the Skill of any player playing outside his normal position for this match.

Overall Skill		Opponent Skill		Morale		Fitness		Home Advantage		Match Factor
61	−	67	+	19	+	18	+	3	=	51

If your MF is more than zero, add 1 to your dice rolls. If it is less than zero, you must subtract 1.

Referee's Watch

15	30	45	60	75	90

League Table

Put the teams in order of points.
If two teams have the same number of points, the one with the best
Goal Difference comes higher.
If they have the same Goal Difference, put them in order of Goals For.

Position	Team name	Goals For	Goals Against	Goal Difference	Points
1					
2					
3					
4					
5					
6					
7					
8					
9					
10					

Win = 3 points
Draw = 1 point
Lose = 0 points

Goal Difference = Goals For – Goals Against

Match Sheet: Saturday 12th

Hardwick City ☐ **vs** ☐ **Bridgford City**

Team Selection

No.	Position	Player name	Skill	Injuries, cards
2	Goalkeeper			
3	Defender			
4	Defender			
5	Def/Mid			
6	Def/Mid			
7	Midfielder			
8	Midfielder			
9	Mid/Att			
10	Mid/Att			
11	Attacker			
12	Attacker			

NB subtract 2 from the Skill of any player playing outside his normal position for this match.

Overall Skill		Opponent Skill		Morale		Fitness		Home Advantage		Match Factor
☐	—	☐	+	☐	+	☐	+	3	=	☐

If your MF is more than zero, add 1 to your dice rolls. If it is less than zero, you must subtract 1.

Referee's Watch

15	30	45	60	75	90

League Table

Put the teams in order of points.
If two teams have the same number of points, the one with the best Goal Difference comes higher.
If they have the same Goal Difference, put them in order of Goals For.

Position	Team name	Goals For	Goals Against	Goal Difference	Points
1					
2					
3					
4					
5					
6					
7					
8					
9					
10					

Win = 3 points
Draw = 1 point
Lose = 0 points

Goal Difference = Goals For – Goals Against

Match Sheet: Saturday 19th

Gunthorpe United ☐ vs ☐ **Hardwick City**

Team Selection

No.	Position	Player name	Skill	Injuries, cards
2	Goalkeeper			
3	Defender			
4	Defender			
5	Def/Mid			
6	Def/Mid			
7	Midfielder			
8	Midfielder			
9	Mid/Att			
10	Mid/Att			
11	Attacker			
12	Attacker			

NB subtract 2 from the Skill of any player playing outside his normal position for this match.

Overall Skill	Opponent Skill	Morale	Fitness	Home Advantage	Match Factor
☐ −	☐ +	☐ +	☐ −	3 =	☐

If your MF is more than zero, add 1 to your dice rolls. If it is less than zero, you must subtract 1.

Referee's Watch

15	30	45	60	75	90

League Table

Put the teams in order of points.
If two teams have the same number of points, the one with the best Goal Difference comes higher.
If they have the same Goal Difference, put them in order of Goals For.

Position	Team name	Goals For	Goals Against	Goal Difference	Points
1					
2					
3					
4					
5					
6					
7					
8					
9					
10					

Win = 3 points
Draw = 1 point
Lose = 0 points

Goal Difference = Goals For – Goals Against

Match Sheet: Saturday 26th

Hardwick City ☐ **vs** ☐ **Woodborough County**

Team Selection

No.	Position	Player name	Skill	Injuries, cards
2	Goalkeeper			
3	Defender			
4	Defender			
5	Def/Mid			
6	Def/Mid			
7	Midfielder			
8	Midfielder			
9	Mid/Att			
10	Mid/Att			
11	Attacker			
12	Attacker			

NB subtract 2 from the Skill of any player playing outside his normal position for this match.

Overall Skill	Opponent Skill	Morale	Fitness	Home Advantage	Match Factor

$$\boxed{} - \boxed{} + \boxed{} + \boxed{} + 3 = \boxed{}$$

If your MF is more than zero, add 1 to your dice rolls. If it is less than zero, you must subtract 1.

Referee's Watch

15	30	45	60	75	90

League Table

Put the teams in order of points.
If two teams have the same number of points, the one with the best
Goal Difference comes higher.
If they have the same Goal Difference, put them in order of Goals For.

Position	Team name	Goals For	Goals Against	Goal Difference	Points
1					
2					
3					
4					
5					
6					
7					
8					
9					
10					

Win = 3 points
Draw = 1 point
Lose = 0 points

Goal Difference = Goals For – Goals Against

Match Sheet: Saturday 3rd

Lambley Rovers ☐ vs ☐ Hardwick City

Team Selection

No.	Position	Player name	Skill	Injuries, cards
2	Goalkeeper			
3	Defender			
4	Defender			
5	Def/Mid			
6	Def/Mid			
7	Midfielder			
8	Midfielder			
9	Mid/Att			
10	Mid/Att			
11	Attacker			
12	Attacker			

NB subtract 2 from the Skill of any player playing outside his normal position for this match.

Overall Skill	Opponent Skill	Morale	Fitness	Home Advantage	Match Factor
☐ −	☐ +	☐ +	☐ −	3 =	☐

If your MF is more than zero, add 1 to your dice rolls. If it is less than zero, you must subtract 1.

Referee's Watch | 15 | 30 | 45 | 60 | 75 | 90 |

League Table

Put the teams in order of points.
If two teams have the same number of points, the one with the best Goal Difference comes higher.
If they have the same Goal Difference, put them in order of Goals For.

Position	Team name	Goals For	Goals Against	Goal Difference	Points
1					
2					
3					
4					
5					
6					
7					
8					
9					
10					

Win = 3 points
Draw = 1 point
Lose = 0 points

Goal Difference = Goals For – Goals Against

Fact Sheet

Budget: £ *7* million

Fixture List

Date	Home /Away	Opponents	Result	
Saturday 15th	H	Lowdham Athletic	1	1
Saturday 22nd	A	Oxton Wanderers	2	3
Saturday 29th	H	Papplewick Town	2	4
Saturday 5th	A	Gonalston City		
Saturday 12th	H	Bridgford City		
Saturday 19th	A	Gunthorpe United		
Saturday 26th	H	Woodborough County		
Saturday 3rd	A	Lambley Rovers		
Saturday 10th	H	Epperstone Town		

Morale: *10*

Fitness: *18*

Clues and Equipment

*Maps 2 halves of paper
Wire Top Flight New
Sponser*

Squad Details

Player	Position	Skill	Injuries, cards, special skills
Jamie Coates	Goalkeeper	5	
Rob Rose	Goalkeeper	5	
	Goalkeeper		
Steve Fitzgerald	Defender	5	
Joe Fry	Defender	4	
Antek Bobak	Defender	5	
Ricky Neville	Defender	4	
Carlos de Carvalho	Defender	6	
	Defender		
	Defender		
Will Frost	Midfielder	5	
Michael Hurley	Midfielder	5	
Dmitri Duval	Midfielder	4	
Anthony Bostock	Midfielder	5	
Klaus Wehnert	Midfielder	6	
John Hoggart	Midfielder	4	
	Midfielder		
	Midfielder		
Ben Parker	Attacker	5	
Salvatore Duce	Attacker	4	
Ian Leslie	Attacker	5	
Jed Stevens	Attacker	5	
Toby Wood	Attacker	6	
	Attacker		
	Attacker		

Remember, if a player is sent off, he must miss the next match as well.

Acknowledgements

Thank you to all the people who helped play-test the book:

Carol Attenburgh, Ashley Nicol, Jane Forrester, Lisa Martin, Heather Cunningham, Greg Smith, Kathleen Meaney, Kerr Gibson, Paul Hunter, George McMillan (all from the English Department, Portobello High School, Edinburgh); Patrick Baker, Jamie Baker, Adie Summerscales, Simon Figures, Nicola Birtwistle, Geoff Sheldon, the real Ben Parker and the real Will Frost.

And a special thanks to James Spackman, without whom this book wouldn't have been started.

www.bigmatchmanager.com

www.bloomsbury.com